Colin Macpherson was bc
He has lived and worked i:
has been a physicist, a teac.
consultant, a farmer, a boatbuilder, an inventor, and an aid
worker. He is also the author of several textbooks and
software packages, as well as being a successful freelance
writer, editor, and publisher. He has a PhD in mathematical
modelling, but still doesn't know what he wants to be when
he grows up. He has lived on the Queensland coast for
many years. This is his third novel.

Other novels by Colin Macpherson

The Tide Turners

The Holy Well

THE BOATBUILDER'S NOSE

Colin Macpherson

Central Queensland
UNIVERSITY
PRESS

First published in 2009 by Central Queensland University Press
P.O. Box 1615, Rockhampton, Queensland 4700, Australia
www.cqunipress.com.au

National Library of Australia
Cataloguing-in-Publication entry:

Macpherson, Colin R. (Colin Robert), 1948-
The boatbuilder's nose / Colin Macpherson.

ISBN: 978 1 921274 10 7 (pbk.)

Smell – Fiction.

A823.3

Cover photograph by Maggy Macpherson
Cover art and typesetting by Designs to Print
Set in 12.1/17pt Adobe Caslon Pro
Printed and bound by Lightning Source Inc.

To Maggy, Lok, Al, and Chrissy;
boatbuilders everywhere;
and most dogs.

Chapter 1

The speaker on the right of the steering wheel still worked. *…and the wind blows heavy on the booorrrderrr line*, Bob Dylan's voice sang – with Derek accompanying him. He punched at the grill on the left, it'd be good to have a bit more volume, but the left speaker remained silent – it was buggered. *"Remember me to the one who lives there,"* he crooned along with his sixties hero as the yacht club gate rolled open. *"For she once was…"*

"Ay Derek, over 'ere."

Dylan didn't worry about the interruption of course – he was thousands of miles away: on tour or sleeping or sailing or rooting. Derek pretended not to mind either: *"…a true love of myyynnne,"* he sang at the top of his voice as he pulled up in front of his skinny assistant, and turned off the engine.

"How long've you been here?" Derek asked, without making a move to get out of the van.

"Since seven, like you said."

"Yeah, well I've been up since five-thirty putting the final coat of epoxy on the hatch covers back at the workshop, so don't go getting critical about me being late or I'll have ya for fuckin' breakfast." Jono looked shocked; his boss was never aggressive towards him, maybe with other people but never him. Derek stared at the teenager for a few seconds – his eyes squinting, his mouth closed tight – and then he winked.

"Oh geez, Derek," Jono said, embarrassed. "Shit!"

"Right, let's get the clamps off the rubbing strip timber and see how your hooked scarphs have held," Derek said, now shifting into his usual, serious-business mode as he slid open the side door of the old Ford van.

Jono stepped towards the opening; the blue letters on the right simply read 'ler' and 'der' – all that remained of 'Derek Sadler' on the top and 'Boatbuilder' on the bottom; the phone number – with its accompanying rust – had slid away with the door. Without speaking, he took the long extension cord off its hook with one hand, and reached for the power drill with the other. Derek was already walking towards the two long strips of dressed timber being supported by the dozen or so bricks lying next to the large steel cradle. Inside the cradle, standing high above the ground, was the elegant thirty-foot wooden boat, *Valkyrie*. Derek looked up for a moment at the vessel's gold-leaf-and-mahogany name board.

"Did you know that the Valkyrie were handmaidens of the god Odin in ancient Scandinavian mythology?" Jono called from behind.

"Did you know that you didn't put any plastic sheet between one of these joins and the clamping off-cut, and that if there's any glue underneath that's oozed out you're gunna be doing a lot of careful cutting and grinding – and bloody time wasting?"

"Oh shit!" the boy said, hurrying forward. "Look! I did all the others." He pointed. "I don't know why I missed that one."

Derek glanced at his apprentice and nodded, a slight grin on his lips. Jono was a good lad – smart, quick to learn, and dedicated to becoming one of the more highly-skilled tradesmen in his chosen field. Everyone has lapses in their concentration – especially when trying to work to a pleading boat-owner's launch deadline – still, the boy would never become a true craftsman if his teacher-and-employer didn't make some issue of mistakes like this, small as they might be.

"Well, you have a think about why," Derek said as he picked up a rectangular piece of black polythene from under the cradle and held it out to Jono, "then it probably won't happen again."

Jono took the piece of plastic from his boss, and frowned – thinking hard. He then spun around. "Oh geez, it was that old guy from this boat," he said, pointing at the tired fibreglass yacht on the corroded trailer next to *Valkyrie*.

"What, Slinky Robinson? What did he do?"

"Oh, you know how he just wants to talk all the fuckin' time while you're tryin' to work. Yesterday, I was just puttin' the clamps on that join – the last one before I knocked off. Anyway, I'd put some polythene on one side, put the off-cut over it, had the clamp in place, and was about to do the other side, when the old guy asks me to give him a hand getting his new water tank in place. He was standin' right behind me when he spoke – frightened the shit out of me."

Derek started removing the clamps. "Here, you do the other one." He indicated with his chin. "But I'm still listenin' – work while you talk."

The apprentice followed his instructions. "Anyway, I stopped what I was doin' and went to have a look at what he was goin' on about. He said it'd only take five minutes but I could see it'd be more like fuckin' fifty, so I told him I'd have to get back to my own job first – before the glue started to go off. He just kept talkin' while I was tryin' to pick up where I'd got up to, and…"

Derek stopped what he was doing and looked up. "And what?"

"And I forgot to insert the plastic."

The older man now stood up, a clamp in his hand. "So what have you learned from this bit of reflection?"

"That you finish what you're doin' before doin' something else."

Derek nodded. "Especially if it involves epoxy," he said, referring to the resin-and-hardener mix that is the basis of so much modern boat work. "Because, once mixed…"

"Epoxy waits for no man," Jono completed. "…or woman," he added.

"Or woman," Derek confirmed.

At morning 'smoko' Derek was quickly scanning through *The Courier Mail*. He liked to keep abreast of both national and international events but now wasn't the time for any in-depth reading – he might have a chance for that at lunchtime, if some fucker didn't come over while he was eating his sandwich and ask for advice or help. He stopped browsing for a moment and sipped the hot black tea from the vacuum-flask lid that also served as a cup. Mary's tea always tasted better than his own – he could never figure out why; there couldn't be any mystery about dangling teabags in a flask of hot water, surely. Mary. He smiled. She'd been fast asleep when he got up this morning – he was always quiet on such occasions. Just before he left the room he had looked back at the bed, and had paused. Her face was turned toward him, and her lower cheek was resting not on the pillow but on her hands, which were held together, palm to palm, in the way that little children are taught to pray. She had looked truly beautiful

– as beautiful as when they'd got married fifteen years earlier: dark eyebrows, long mouth, button nose. He had stood at the door in quiet admiration. Then she had farted and rolled over. He had left pretty well straight away after that.

"What are you grinning about?" It was Jono's voice.

Derek closed his newspaper as his consciousness twanged back to the present. "Nothin'", he said. "Let's get back to *Valkyrie*. We've still got a lot to do if the owner's gunna be goin' on his fuckin' holiday cruise at the end of the week." As he stood up he had one last vision of Mary as she had been that morning, and he wondered why they hadn't had sex for so long. *Both workin' too hard*, he thought as he threw out the remnants of his tea onto the grass.

It was six-thirty and already dark before he drove up the dirt track towards the old wooden Queenslander house that was set on the ten acres of bushland that he and Mary owned. Rifkin, their large, dappled mongrel – a result of canine multiculturalism is how Mary described him – came running down the track barking, as he did every time the van came home.

"G'day Rifkin," Derek called from the driver's seat as he parked the van under the corrugated-iron roof that they called 'the garage'. After getting out, he spent a few seconds patting the dog before deciding to go and have a quick look at the hatch covers and several other jobs that he had at various stages of completion in the adjoining workshop – a similar pole-and-roof affair but with wooden walls on three sides and two huge metal doors on the remaining side, for getting boats in and out of. He had just flicked on the light switch when he heard a familiar sound.

"Dadddeee!" his six year-old called while scuttling down the back stairs of the house. Rifkin picked up on the excitement and barked several times before trailing off into a 'wooo wooo wooo' sort of dog talk.

"So, little Harry, how was school today?" Derek asked, his youngest now in his arms as he lifted him onto a clear bit of bench space.

"We made a fish and I got pushed over by Francine MacIntyre at lunchtime and Eddy my friend vomited up a chocolate frog and Missus Stewart said my story about Mister Wiggle The Worm was 'excellent'. 'Eks-sal-lent'." He took a breath and smiled.

Derek laughed. What a joy children were.

"Daddy, you're not going to do more work now, are you? I want you to come and look at my fish."

Derek's smile diminished a little as he glanced over at the table where he had strips of timber laminate clamped against a moulding piece – it was to be a new tiller for a regular client, and he'd said he'd have it ready by the end of the week; it'd mean shaping it tonight so there'd be enough time for the several layers of polyurethane varnish to set in time. *Fuck!* he thought. "Tell you what Harry, you go and get your fish ready, and say to Mum that I'll be fifteen minutes. I have to make a start here – I'll have to come back after dinner as it is."

The boy's expression changed, and he lowered himself from the bench. Rifkin followed him towards the door. Derek paused for a moment before walking over to his tool cabinet to look for his spoke-shave; but then he turned and called towards the house, "And you can tell me about the worm story later on too – I'll look forward to that."

Half an hour later, he was still spoke-shaving the tiller when his older son wandered into the workshop. "Mum says she can't hold dinner any longer, and that if you don't come right now we're going to eat anyway." He stood, a bored expression on his face, waiting for a reply.

Derek looked up from the tiller, the beauty of its curves and alternating strips of light and dark timbers now becoming apparent – but it was obviously of no interest to the fourteen year-old. "G'day Tim," Derek said as he glanced across to the old clock above the main workbench. "Shit! Have I been here that long?" He would've liked to ask his son about his day, or to maybe exchange some thoughts about football or music or some other topic that interested the boy, but Tim's demeanor showed that he just wanted an answer about dinner, nothing else. "You guys eat without me – I shouldn't be too much longer,"

Derek said. The boy turned. "I just have to sand this tiller and then give it a first coat of varnish." As his son walked away he added, "I was going to do it later but I've just remembered that I have to prepare a quote for a big job by the morning; tell Mum that will you?"

"Yeah, okay," the teenager said quietly without looking back.

It was close to nine o'clock when Derek finally stepped through the back door into the kitchen. Mary was sitting across in the eating area, a pile of student papers on the table in front of her. "Your dinner's in the microwave," she said without looking up, "but I can't say what it's going to taste like."

He stared at her as she pulled a paper from the pile, ticking and crossing and scribbling on it in what appeared to be furious speed; and then he walked over to the microwave and popped it open. Inside, a T-bone steak sat in its cold juices on one of the large plates that they'd got off his brother as a wedding present. The steak had completely lost any remnant of what would've been its lovely sizzling aroma, but it would probably heat up okay – as would the pile of green peas next to it – but the chips would be soft and greasy, the life gone from them – which was just about how he felt at the moment. "I'm sorry Mary," he said, "I just had to get that tiller varnished before…"

"I really don't want to hear about it," she interrupted

while running a red line through some innocent kid's piece of prose. She then looked up and glared at him.

"I think you should go into the lounge room and see whose been waiting for you." Derek frowned. "Don't worry, it's not another one of your customers," she added, the venom almost spurting from her lips.

He opened his mouth to speak but decided against it, not while she was in this state; so he walked into the adjoining room. The television was on – with the sound turned down a lot, thank God. It was showing that stupid, city woman who constantly blabbed away about her sex life. *Horse face*, he thought, as he looked away from the screen. Stretched out on the couch was little Harry, fast asleep. He was lying on his stomach with his head turned towards the TV. His right arm was hanging down, and on the floor, next to his open hand, was a cardboard fish with bits of aluminium foil and coloured paper stuck all over it like scales. It had a big multi-coloured eye and an equally-impressive smile. Derek sat down next to his little boy's head which he gently stroked with one of his sawdust-covered hands. He leaned over and picked up the fish. It was quite a work of art, he thought, not real bad for a six year-old – and it had obviously taken a fair bit of time to make. After examining the fish for a few minutes he placed it on the nearby coffee table. He then stood up and carefully lifted his limp son to his chest, and while holding the boy's head to his shoulder, he walked down the passageway towards the bedrooms.

He was still humming the half remembered and half made up lullaby tune when he quietly closed Harry's bedroom door. As the latch clicked, he wondered why he was humming at all – the boy had already been asleep for goodness sake. Another case of being too late, he thought. It seemed like he was doing everything too late these days, always trying to catch up but never quite getting there. It was the work of course; he was good at what he did and everyone in the area knew it, and so everyone wanted him to do their boat repairs. But no-one had any money, fuckit – or so it seemed – and he was a crap businessman anyway, always doing favours and taking pity on some poor bastard who needed his help. He still loved what he did – ever since he'd been an apprentice like young Jono – but it just ate into his waking hours like a great white shark munching through a mackerel. Yet what the fuck else could he do? He had to earn money – food, school, the mortgage, the business – Mary's part-time teaching salary wouldn't pay for it all.

He decided to have a shower before eating – Mary seemed to be sensitive to mahogany dust, and even though he'd removed his overalls before coming inside, he knew there was still some on his hands, and it was probably in his hair as well. Besides, she might've calmed down by the time he'd finished – it'd be nice to have a friendly chat with her; it'd been a while.

On the way to the bathroom he noticed light coming from under the door of his older son's room. He knocked and waited.

"What?" the boy's voice called, not friendly.

Derek opened the door. Tim was sitting at the small, finely-crafted desk his father had made for him several years earlier – 'Every high-schooler should have a decent homework desk,' he could remember having said to his grinning firstborn. The teenager wasn't grinning now, however. "What is it?" he said, swinging round on his chair and looking up from the keyboard that lay across his outstretched thighs.

Derek glanced at the monitor on the desk, it's blinking cursor signalling a point halfway through some text. His son glared at him and hit a key; the screen went black. "Sorry," Derek said, "I wasn't reading anything." He paused, feeling uncomfortable. "I just thought I'd stick my head in and see how things were going." He tried to sound cheery.

"I'm working," Tim said, turning back towards the screen.

"What, on school work?" his father responded with what he thought was the same friendly tone, but feeling some rising annoyance.

"No," his son replied, without turning round.

"Well what is it?" Derek could hear the edge on his

own voice.

"Just something I'm doing," Tim said, taking his hands off the keyboard and lowering his head but still not turning round.

"Listen! Would you mind looking at me when you speak – I didn't bring you up to be a rude little bastard ya know." Tim pushed himself around and stared in the direction of his father, but not into his eyes. "It seems like I haven't seen you for more than a few minutes over the last month – I just wanted to have a friendly chat."

"Oh, is that what this is?" Tim said as he briefly locked eyes with his father.

"Geez, I don't know what's got up your arse Timothy but I tell you what, it's getting very hard to talk to you lately." The boy looked away, clearly not wanting to engage in any further conversation. Derek shook his head and headed for the door. "And get off the fucking Internet, it's costing us too much money," he said without looking back.

"I'm not on the 'fucking Internet'," Tim replied.

Derek turned, his son was typing. He paused for a moment, his anger mixing with sadness and confusion. No words came, so he left the room, closing the door less gently than when he'd opened it.

He felt a bit better after having a shower – clean and fresh and determined to turn disaster into success, at least with his wife. With this in mind, and wearing his new red pyjama shorts and a white T-shirt, both of which Mary had given him for his birthday a month ago, he jumped through the kitchen doorway. "*Da-dah*," he sang, announcing himself and spreading his arms in a flourish. But his attempt at levity was wasted; Mary wasn't there. Rifkin raised his head from his second most favourite sleeping spot in the corner but then dropped it down again when he saw that there was no food involved. A smaller pile of student essays was still on the table – those that Mary had already corrected, it appeared, and there was also a sheet of A4 under her coffee cup, with a note in large, black, marker-pen writing. 'Dagmar rang, has had to take Brian to hospital – bad stomach pains – asked me to mind other kids. Don't know when I'll be back.' There was no 'Love, Mary' or even just 'Mary'; just 'Don't know when I'll be back' – and a full-stop. Derek sighed and then walked across to Rifkin. "*Da-dah*," he exclaimed for a second time, repeating the hand thing as well. The dog looked at him and then got up off the floor and walked into the lounge room, no doubt heading for his basket, his most preferred sleeping location. *Not even the fucking dog*, Derek thought to himself as he wandered over to the microwave.

He was still sitting at the table two hours later – the plate pushed to one side, and his pocket calculator and various price lists on the other side. In front of him was his 'quotes' notebook. He put down his pen when he heard the familiar sound of Mary's car driving up the track. Rifkin came running from the lounge room and nosed open the slightly ajar kitchen door – the back half of his body staying inside, tail wagging. A minute or so passed, and then Mary entered.

"What are you doing still up?" she asked as she placed the papers under her arm on top of those already on the table.

"I had this quote to do – remember? It's for a little sailing cat." Rifkin suddenly looked around from sniffing Mary's legs, his ears pricked – he knew that word. They both smiled, but the moment quickly passed.

"Well, I hope you've added a much higher margin than you usually do, or the kids are going to be attending school barefooted."

"What's that supposed to mean?" he said.

"It's supposed to mean that the last small boat you built almost ended up costing us money; you could've been making three times as much on repairs instead of doing a favour for that blasted doctor in town – you barely broke even on the job, and you don't even know the man."

"Doctor Jacobs? Of course I know him, he stitched up my hand after that accident three years ago."

Mary gave him a look of mild contempt. "You know what I mean," she replied.

It wasn't worth pursuing. Derek didn't want to get

into an argument about what it meant to 'know' someone – especially not with his English-teacher wife. But she was right about that job, the material costs had gone through the roof after he'd given the quote – and some of the special features on the boat had taken him a lot longer than he'd estimated. He'd been a fool to give such a totally fixed quote in the first place, but Jacobs had insisted – formal contract, the whole thing. It wasn't the way Derek usually worked.

"Anyway, I've added another ten percent on top of the usual, and made it subject to price increases in materials costs." She didn't reply but walked over to the sink and began to fill the kettle with water. "So how's Dagmar's little fella?" he asked, attempting to move away from any further confrontation.

"He seems okay now," she replied. "She thinks that he probably ate some pellets out of their dog's bowl. But at the time she wasn't sure what was going on – he was just screaming with a sore stomach. Apparently they could hear him at Mendelson's farm. Old Missus Mendelson telephoned Dagmar and asked her whether she was sacrificing Brian to the god Odin – you know, Dagmar being Norwegian – sarcastic old biddy."

"That's the second time someone's mentioned that name to me today," Derek said, his eyebrows angled slightly. "Amazing."

"What, 'biddy'?" Mary said as she walked over to the pantry.

"No, 'Odin'," he replied. "So what was it – with little whatsisname?"

"Oh, the young intern at the hospital examined him and said it was gas. They gave him some stuff to drink, he did a big shit, and then he seemed fine. They took a faeces sample just in case, but told her to take him home." She reached for a mug in the cupboard and then turned to him. "Do you want a cup of tea?"

"Yeah, that'd be nice," Derek said. He was a bit surprised too; not because of what she said but because of the subtle change in expression on his wife's face – the tiredness and grumpiness giving way to something more...girlie.

"Why don't you hop into bed and I'll bring it to you in there."

She had her back to him as she turned off the kettle, and her voice was still matter-of-fact like, but Derek knew there was something going on. "I'm on my way," he said without hesitating.

He lay propped up with one of Mary's pillows as well as his own two – mug of black tea in one hand and turning the pages of *The Courier Mail* with the other. She was in the bathroom, humming; he hadn't heard that for a while. She had handed him the mug and then, just for a few seconds, had stroked his moustache – straightening the sides like she used to do when they were younger – and her fingertips had briefly run across his lips. They hadn't had sex for…how long had it been…a month? Maybe even more. He took a sip of the hot liquid and then put the mug on the bedside table, next to the pile of books that he one-day intended to read. For the moment, though, this article about the Sphinx in Egypt looked interesting…his dad had been to Egypt during the war; he remembered the story about the Arab boys and how…a boat came into view…there was a woman on the deck waving, she wasn't wearing anything above her waist…such nice brown…

"You're not asleep are you?" Mary's voice penetrated his unconscious. The brown woman disappeared.

"Wha…oh…sorry. Nah, I was just dozing." His eyelids opened briefly but then closed again.

"Derek! Look at me." Her voice seemed loud.

He opened his eyes again, and he now used all his mental strength to keep them that way. Mary was lying on her back with the blankets folded a fair way down. She was naked except for her white panties – which he could just see the top of. She knew that he liked to start making love while she still had her panties on, that he liked to remove them himself as things got underway. He rolled over next to her and kissed one of her nipples, and proceeded to suck on it – gently noticing how quickly it became hard. Mary sighed and began to stroke his head, and he placed his hand on the soft, cotton material that covered her crotch.

He remembered how she used to have all her pubic hair waxed away – that was when they were first married. He'd really liked it, but then things had slowed down…slowed right down…slowed…sucking…stroking. There was that boat again, and that brown woman – Polynesian, like he'd seen on that travel photo the other day. She had white panties on too – with stars…so many stars, all in the night sky…but now they were twinkling out… Bye bye stars…

"Jesus, Derek."

He heard Mary's voice coming from far away.

"I'd get more out of a banana."

He felt her pushing him over, just like when he'd been snoring. Was she angry? Had he been snoring? It'd be okay now, he was on his side. "Night," he said almost unintelligibly, from some other universe.

Next morning Mary was already out of bed by the time he woke up. After shaving and washing and dressing he walked down the passageway towards the kitchen. In the lounge room, Harry was sitting cross-legged on the floor watching a kids' program that had some dork prancing around dressed as a dinosaur. "Hey little fella," Derek said. "Watchyadoin'?"

"Watching TV," Harry said, obviously focused on whatever the dinosaur was up to.

"Hey, Harry, I saw your fish last night – it is really well made – I liked it a lot." Then as an afterthought, "I'm sorry

I was a bit late in getting to you."

"That's okay," the boy replied without looking around. But then he did turn around, pointing at the screen and laughing – the dinosaur had fallen over into a cream cake. Derek snorted and smiled, but when Harry turned back to the screen he walked on to the kitchen.

Mary was sitting at the table spooning cereal into her mouth while marking papers.

"Good morning Sweetie," he said. "I thought you'd finished all those last night."

"No, I should've though," she replied, not taking her eyes off her work.

Derek frowned and wondered why she had that annoyed tone in her voice. He nodded and walked over to the toaster, a massive yawn stretching his face as he cut a slice of bread. "God! I must've been tired last night – I slept more than like a log – like a fuckin' timber mill."

"Yes, well, that's good isn't it?" she said, and then called to Harry to get ready because they were leaving soon. "I told Dagmar I'd drop in and see her before going to school," she added.

"So it'll just be me and Timmy this morning," he said. "I'll be a bit late for work and drive him to school – surprise him."

"Not today you won't," she said, standing and placing the papers in her satchel. "He left early for the school camp. Eric's dad came by and picked him up – he had a whole carload of kids."

"School camp?" Derek said, as Harry ran into the room.

"I told you about it last week – and it's all that Tim has been talking about for ages. He'll be gone until Friday night." She shook her head. "Come on Harry, we have to go – say goodbye to Daddy."

Five minutes later Derek was alone with his toast. Yet for some reason he didn't feel hungry. He sat for a moment idly stroking his moustache, and then he remembered the previous night, when Mary had done the same thing to him. He heard a scratching sound at the back door, and then Rifkin walked in from outside. He looked at the dog. "You know, Rifkin, I'm a fuckin' idiot," he said. "A real, fucking idiot."

He had just finished spraying a two-pot varnish on the hatch covers for *Valkyrie* when Jono drove up the track in his old Holden ute. The nineteen year-old could see that the polytarp screens were closed in the area near the workshop where they did the spraying of small components – sort of like a big, four-sided, shower-curtain affair – so he stopped someway back, to avoid making dust.

"G'day boss," he said as he pulled apart two velcroed sections of the hanging blue plastic and poked his head inside.

Derek lifted the filter mask from his face and winced

as he realized that not all the varnish vapour had settled yet. He held his breath while giving the three curved wooden box-top structures a final perusal, and then walked towards the opening. "Okay, that's done", he said with the remnants of air still in his lungs. "Let's get down to the yacht club."

Jono paused to look at the hatch covers while his employer pushed past him. Even though he rarely commented on it these days, he was always impressed with the quality of Derek's workmanship – often stunned. It was one of the reasons he stayed with him even though the pay was crap – the guy was a master. "That Tasmanian oak and meranti looks really good together," he called to Derek who was already in the garage loading something into the van.

"Bring the spray gun here and cover the compressor please Jono," the older man replied. "We've got a lot to do today."

On the way to Ross Harbour – where the yacht club was located – Jono just stared out of the side window. Derek hadn't turned on the radio as he usually did, and Jono's couple of attempts to start a conversation had been met with short, perfunctory responses. They were passing the area where every second house seemed to have a large mango tree in its front yard – some already bearing young fruits – when Derek spoke.

"You still hanging out with the MacLaren girl, Jono?"

he asked.

Jono looked across at his boss. "Nah, we split up months ago," he said. "I'm goin' out with Wendy Butler now."

"What, Andy Butler's daughter?"

"Yeah, that's right."

"I thought she was in Brisbane."

"That's her sister; Wendy's the younger one." They drove in silence past several more mango trees, and then Jono added, "This one's gettin' to be kinda special."

Derek took his eyes off the road for a moment and looked across at his apprentice. "Treat her right then, Jono, won'cha?" He looked back at the road as he flicked the indicator for the turn-off to the harbour. "Sometimes we don't know how lucky we are," he added quietly as he changed gears.

Jono was relieved when, later in the morning, Derek seemed to come out of his glum state. They were on opposite sides of the boat, each standing on one of the trestles they'd set up the previous day. Both were tapping wooden plugs into the countersunk screw holes of the rubbing strips when Derek started to whistle. Jono waited for a moment and then joined in, attempting to harmonize with the melody.

Derek stopped. "What the fuck is that?" he called,

unseen, from the other side of the boat.

"It's the chorus to that Neil Young song you're always humming."

There was a few seconds of silence. "Bullshit!" came the reply. "I made that tune up ages ago."

Another pause. "No you didn't, I've heard it heaps of times – my uncle's got it on CD."

"Really?"

"Yeah, it's called *Cinnamon Girl*, he wrote it way before I was born."

"What, your uncle wrote it?"

"No, Neil Young…smartarse."

Derek chuckled. He was feeling a bit better about himself now, having resolved that he'd go home early today and surprise Mary – and buy her some flowers from that roadside stall on the way. He'd get something for Harry too. In anticipation of this he moved seamlessly from banter to seriousness. "When did you last sharpen your handplane blade?" he asked Jono as a prelude to telling the lad that he would be left alone to cut and finish all the plugs later in the day, once the glue had set. But as his offsider was replying, Derek suddenly became aware of another person standing just below and behind him. It was the old man who owned the boat that was normally next door.

"Oh geez, Slinky!" Derek said in surprise. "How long have you been standing there?"

"A few minutes; I didn't want to interrupt you."

"So what's happening? Is your boat in the water?"

The old man wrinkled his nose as he looked up at Derek. "Well I was supposed to launch it early this morning but when I got it on the ramp I did a final check of the new water tank I put in yesterday and found all this bloody water coming from somewhere. The plumbing looks okay, so I think it's the welding. I'm going to have to bring the boat back here and get the blasted tank out again and see what's going on."

"Well, that's a bit of a bummer," Derek replied turning back to his rubbing strip. He felt some sympathy for Slinky, but if you owned a boat then this was the sort of thing that happened – it was in their nature. Besides, he had a lot of his own work to complete if he was going to leave early, as planned. He couldn't allow himself to get involved in someone else's boat problems – not today.

"Anyway," the old man continued beneath him, "I was wondering if you'd give me a hand in reversing the boat back into its spot here? Jim Henderson was helping me earlier but he had to go to work."

Derek looked around. *Poor old bugger*, he thought. *How can I say no*. "I'll get young Jono to direct you from behind; how's that?"

"Oh, that'd be terrific thanks Derek – your blood's worth bottling," the old man replied. "It'll only be for a few minutes." Derek called across to his apprentice but

Jono was already off the trestle and was walking towards them from the stern of *Valkyrie*.

More than half an hour passed before Derek heard the ancient, club tractor coming up the driveway from the ramp. He was still standing on the trestle but was now leaning over the gunwale of the yacht sanding a section of the deck. He stopped what he was doing and saw that Slinky was driving the tractor, with his boat and trailer in tow, while Jono walked behind. Soon, the apprentice was almost next to Derek – but at ground level – yelling out instructions to the old man who was attempting to reverse the tall keelboat into its narrow, allotted space.

"Left…" Jono called. "No, LEFT," he called even louder as he gesticulated with his arms. Derek grinned. Slinky had been doing this for years but still had trouble getting his boat in place. He put the sander on *Valkyrie*'s deck, deciding that he'd get his apprentice back a lot quicker if he offered to park the trailer himself.

He was in the middle of turning round when he heard a sudden roar come from the tractor motor. It was accompanied by a scream – not a loud call but a scream – from Jono. He still hadn't completed his turn when the plank on which he'd been standing jolted sideways and then apparently disappeared from under his feet. He felt himself falling backwards. This was bad. He realized that if he continued on the same trajectory he wouldn't land on his feet but on his back – not the best way to hit the ground or the section of steel trailer that was probably now under him at some strange angle. He wildly tried to grab at the safety rails of *Valkyrie* but they were already too far away. He saw the sky and for some crazy reason noticed the deepness of the blue. At the same time, he tried to twist his body around so his hands might cushion the inevitable impact. Colour and desperation – such weird partners for a time like this. His next racing thought was about concrete – he knew there was a patch of it somewhere beneath him; and that it had a big eyebolt sticking out of it, for attaching a security chain. Hitting this would not be a good thing.

Derek *heard* the impact of his head rather than feel it – a cracking sound like when you fracture a husked coconut with a large hammer – and he caught a glimpse of the eyebolt, only a few centimetres away. He was aware of pain for a moment but this disappeared as his vision went black. Also, Jono's voice – which had been loud at first – seemed to travel away from him at some enormous speed, and then it was gone. The last thing he noticed before being totally consumed by darkness, was a smell – it was…honeysuckle, he thought.

Chapter 2

Mary could see that this was going to be an enjoyable period – her year-ten English class were a good bunch of kids, and the two teams had done a lot of preparation. And now the debate had begun: 'Should the federal government allow more refugees to settle in Australia?' Everyone was laughing because the boy standing in front of the class had just started his team's argument with a joke. She was sitting at the back of the room, near the door, when she saw the principal, Emily Riccardi, enter. At first she thought that Emily had come to listen – having said yesterday that she'd try to attend. But the look on her face was solemn, not the usual optimistic smile and cheery glow. High concern and sympathy, that's what Mary saw in the principal's ashen face, and it made her shudder.

"Come outside for a minute, Mary," Emily whispered, her hand on Mary's shoulder. "Mister Hounslow will stand in for you."

Mary looked at the principal and then focused on the man behind her, a supply teacher who often filled in for staff who were away sick or on school excursions. She didn't say a word but stood and indicated to the boy speaking up front that he should continue despite the minor disturbance that the entry of the two other teachers had caused. She then quickly left the room. Emily was behind her, and it was she who closed the door.

"Mary, there's been an accident at the yacht club," she said as she reached out and held both of Mary's arms while looking into her eyes. "Derek fell from a trestle and hit his head on some concrete." Mary's eyes widened and her mouth opened, but before her question – *the* question – came out, Emily answered. "He's alive, but unconscious. The ambulance took him to the local hospital first but they almost immediately transferred him to St Vincent's in Trelborough. He's probably just getting there now."

Mary blinked and then held a hand to her mouth. "Oh," was all she said as she looked from side to side. Two year-eight students on their way down the corridor hovered nearby. Emily gave them a steely look and their hovering ceased.

"I'll drive you there if you like," she continued.

Mary's moment of apparent confusion ended abruptly. "No, I'll go myself, but I'd be grateful if you would arrange for someone to pick up Harry from school. Someone he knows – Dagmar Hendersen – phone her and ask her to do it." She began to run down the corridor. "Ask her to keep him until I phone," she said as she disappeared round the corner.

The car park at St V's was close to full. Mary expressed some of her mounting anxiety by driving faster than she should while looking for somewhere to put her Volkswagen beetle – and, uncharacteristically, by swearing. "Where the fucking hell is there a fucking place to put my fucking car?" she yelled as she swerved around the end of yet another full row of vehicles. Then she saw an old man with a walking stick; he was pointing to a place halfway down the row – a sympathetic stranger – an empty space. She nodded in thanks to the old man, and felt a little ashamed about her behaviour.

She passed through the main entrance at a run, and was breathing heavily as the reception desk loomed up in front of her. "My husband, Derek Sadler, was brought here less than an hour ago from Yuragan Hospital – he was unconscious," she called from several metres away. The woman sitting behind the desk appeared to simply look at her. "So where is he?" Mary said, annoyed at the apparent indifference and ineptitude, but then noticing that the woman was typing on a keyboard.

"I'm sorry dear," the lady said "Our system's a bit slow today, but I've put your husband's name in and…here it is: he's out of ED and up on the third floor, east wing." She smiled. It seemed inappropriate.

"Is that a special ward?" Mary asked as she looked back at the sign she'd passed seconds earlier that showed the directions of the various hospital departments and wards.

"It's an intensive-care unit," the woman replied, her expression now more sombre. "Back there to the lifts," she pointed, "and then turn right when you get out and follow the red line on the floor." Mary was already running for the lift before the woman had finished.

"But he's always so careful; ever since his father died in a boatyard twenty years ago – he's always going on about safety…I don't understand." Mary stopped and looked through the large window at her husband's form lying on the bed. His head was heavily bandaged, and he was surrounded by electronic boxes that flashed up numbers and curved lines and vertical bars on their dark screens. Tubes were attached to his arms, feeding liquids into his veins from hanging plastic bags, and others went into his nostrils and into the side of his mouth. In one corner of the room, where the ceiling met the walls, there was a small, black device with a dull red light on top – a video camera. Mary guessed it was sending images of Derek to the nurses' station just near to where she was standing with the white-coated neurosurgeon.

"Yes, well from what I understand, it wasn't his fault at all; some vehicle knocked him off a platform," the doctor said. "But the main thing is that he's alive and that his functions have stabilized. The seizure or whatever it was that he had in the Emergency Department may have been due to the small piece of stone that went through his skull."

Mary turned to him. "But it's all gone now isn't it?"

"Oh yes, we were able to get it out without any trouble. But…"

Mary shivered. "But what?"

The doctor frowned slightly and spoke more slowly – cautiously. "Well, the stone – it was more a triangular sliver that must have broken of something larger – actually entered your husband's brain; just the tip, and like I said, we were lucky enough to remove it without any trouble. However, it did penetrate a short distance." He saw the rising fear on Mary's face, and held up his hand in a gesture of 'but wait'. "The scan shows the possibility – I stress, only the possibility – of the tiniest amount of damage to an area called the rhinencephalon at the base of his brain." He bent his head forward and pointed to an area at the bottom of his own skull – right in the middle at the back where the final bump of hard bone ends and what seems like soft tissue begins. "We can't be sure at this stage but even if there is some damage it will probably only manifest itself as a slight loss of his sense of smell." It's a teeny bit complicated because the stone injury is in the same area that his skull fractured. But there's no pressure on his brain, the paramedics stemmed the blood loss, and his vital signs are looking good. I'm very hopeful that he'll recover completely."

For the first time in the discussion Mary's face showed a measure of relief – small but noticeable. "So…?" she asked.

"So we'll keep him here until he regains consciousness, do some further checks on him, and then – if everything is okay – we'll send him off to one of the wards for a night or two, and then home."

Mary looked into the doctor's eyes – they were green but one was lighter than the other. "When do you think he'll wake up?" she said.

The cautious tone returned to the doctor's voice. "I really can't say, Missus Sadler – it could be an hour; it could be ten hours; maybe longer."

"It's a better sign if it's sooner rather than later though, isn't it?"

"It depends," he replied, and then obviously saw the anxiety return to Mary's face. "Look, I wouldn't worry Missus Sadler; I expect he'll be home with you soon, and as good as new."

Mary stared back through window and nodded.

"You can go and sit with him if you like, or maybe you'd like to go and get something to drink in the cafeteria. He's in the best of care you know. I'll return as soon as I can after he regains consciousness."

Mary looked back at the doctor and for the first time noticed his nametag – 'Richard Barrington'. She knew he'd introduced himself earlier but was equally aware that the name had just passed over her without sticking; her husband's condition was all she'd wanted to know about. She sighed. "Thanks Richard," she said, never having had any time for professional titles. "I'll go and sit with him, and I'll no doubt see you later." She held out her hand. He took it, shook it gently, and then walked away.

She'd been sitting next to Derek for two hours – the sound of his breathing barely audible but the various displays showing that he was in fact alive – when she saw his right hand move. And then his eyes blinked open.

Even as Mary's hand was reaching out for that of her husband, a nurse was in the room. "Hello there," she said, loud and cheerily, "can you tell me your name?"

No part of Derek moved except his eyes. "*Dazzle Wooshinghm*," he seemed to say from a mouth that had been sucked dry of moisture and through lips that seemed to be stuck together with contact cement.

"What did he say?" the nurse asked as she glanced at Mary.

"I think he said, 'Denzel Washington'," Mary replied, smiling. The nurse frowned. She didn't know that Derek was gently squeezing his wife's hand, but Mary noticed it of course, and she felt a sudden wave of relief and happiness pass through her. "Don't worry," she reassured the nurse, "he's behaving quite normally."

After several more questions designed to ascertain Derek's degree of awareness and lucidity, the nurse left to page the doctor. "Sheesh not mush fun," the injured boatbuilder said to his wife.

"She's just doing her job," Mary replied quietly, grateful to everyone in the entire hospital system that her husband was alive and recovering from his potentially disastrous accident – she couldn't care two cents if any one of them had a sense of humour or not.

"An' sheesh god her period," Derek said as he opened and closed his mouth, trying to generate saliva.

Furrows appeared on Mary's brow. "How on Earth do you know that?" she said.

"Because…" Derek attempted to move – to turn and see if there was a glass of water nearby, "Because…ow!… fuck!" He sunk back into the pillows, his face grimacing.

"What's the matter?" Mary asked as she leaned over him, concerned.

"My fucking head is what's the matter," he said, lying dead still and now speaking clearly. "It bloody well hurts."

A short time later, Doctor Barrington arrived. He shone a light in Derek's eyes, got him to move his feet and fingers and arms in various ways, and asked him to focus on his own upright finger as he moved it in different directions. "Excellent," he pronounced. "Everything seems fine." He stood up.

"What about my actual head?" Derek said.

"How do you mean?" the doctor replied.

"It hurts when I turn it."

"In that case don't turn it," Barrington said, but then saw Derek's expression of *oh thanks a lot you dickhead*, and added, "You've suffered a concussion and some internal bruising – your head will be sore for a few days. But the pain should diminish fairly quickly." He gave what Derek perceived as a genuinely sympathetic smile, said he'd see him tomorrow, and after nodding to Mary, turned to leave. As he was about to step from the room, Derek called to him.

"Hey Doc, someone just died around here didn't they? A woman…with her daughter close by."

Barrington stopped; Mary frowned. The nurse who was also in the room opened her mouth, but said nothing. "Why do you say that?" the doctor said as he walked back towards his patient, glancing at the nurse on his way.

Concern appeared on Derek's face. "Well, this is going to sound like I've got a few roos loose in the top paddock, but I can…sort of…smell it."

The three others stared at Derek – still flat on his back and only able to look about by moving his eyes. Barrington spoke first. "What exactly is it that you can smell?" he asked as he sat down on the side of the bed.

"Oh man, this is crazy," Derek replied as he turned his head ever so slightly towards Mary, looking for some sort of reassurance. She took his hand and gave it a squeeze, and he saw the almost imperceptible nod. "Well…just before, I could smell her living body – but then it changed, became sort of…dark; bad. It happened very quickly."

"And why do you say her daughter is with her?" It was the nurse speaking. The others looked at her and then back at Derek.

"Because there is another odour coming from close to the first one," he said, "…distinct and different…but with lots of similarities – and much younger; like the mid twenties."

"Interesting," Barrington said with his lips slightly pursed and his head moving up and down. "Olfactory hallucinations are not unusual with some…" but before he could continue, the nurse interrupted him.

"I'm sorry doctor, but I think I should tell you that just before you came in here, Missus O'Dwyer in IC-5 had a coronary – they weren't able to save her…and her daughter was by her side when it happened." The doctor glared at her – her eyes were wide. "I know I'm not supposed to say anything in front of other patients…" she looked at Derek and Mary, and then back at the doctor, "…but I thought it might help you and Mister Sadler figure out what's happening here."

"A coincidence is what's happening here," he said,

obviously annoyed at his nursing colleague's abandonment of protocol.

"I don't think I'm 'smelling things' – if that's the same as 'seeing things'," Derek said. "For instance, I can smell that you're pissed off – it's come just now – and I can tell you something about the dozen or so other people around here. Most of them I can't even see."

"Derek, hallucinations can appear very real to those having them, and they can be triggered and enhanced by a whole range of situations. For example, the tone of my voice showed that I was…less than pleased," he looked at the nurse, "and that set off a small olfactory hallucination in you that made you think you could smell something different about me – the injury you suffered would support this diagnosis. We'll talk more about it tomorrow." He stood up. Derek turned again to Mary; something passed between them. She looked at the now-smiling doctor, and then at the clearly-worried nurse.

"Just before you go, Richard," she said, and then turned to the nurse. "Please believe that I don't want to embarrass you, but can I ask…are you menstruating?"

Astonishment crossed the face of the young woman in white, quickly followed by concern. "Why in heaven's name do you want to know that?" she said.

It was Mary who looked embarrassed – her ears going pink. "It's just that…before…Derek said to me that you were having your period. You could smell it couldn't you?"

she said, looking at her husband. He nodded, proud of his wife's support in the face of expert opinion.

The nurse swallowed heavily, looked at the doctor – who seemed slightly taken aback by what was happening – and then nodded. "Yes, I am," she said.

There was a momentary pause in the conversation, and then Derek spoke. "There's another nurse – older – who is also having her period; she's passed by the door a few times; and there's another one who…" he seemed uncomfortable.

"Who what?" Mary said.

"Who…ahh…whose in the opposite state," he said.

Mary looked at him with the hint of a smile. "You mean…"

"I mean she's fertile. Horny as hell, actually."

Barrington and Mary looked at each other and then at the nurse. Lines had appeared on her forehead. She stared back and gave a tentative nod. On the bed, Derek had his eyes closed.

After two nights in hospital, another scan, and further meetings with Doctor Barrington, Derek was discharged. It was mid-morning, and he watched from the passenger seat as the shops and offices of Trelborough sped by. Few people were on the streets but this wasn't uncommon for this time of year; already the sun had a bite to it. He'd not spoken more than a few words since getting into the car – had just been sitting and watching. This worried Mary a little – he was normally more talkative – so she was relieved when he did finally say something. "Let's go and have a coffee. Over there." He pointed to a small café up ahead that was wedged between a real estate agency and a chemist shop.

Mary began to pull over. "But you hardly ever have coffee," she said, obviously surprised.

"I know, but it just smells so good – don't you think?"

She looked across at him and noticed that his window was down – just a smidge; but all she could smell was… nothing much…maybe exhaust fumes – certainly not coffee.

They sat at one of the small tables out on the footpath, with Derek adjusting the big umbrella so that they were both shaded from the sun's heat and glare. The last couple of days had been full of surprises for Mary, so she wasn't totally dumbstruck when her husband asked the waitress for a particular *type* of coffee – not the one that most of the other customers were drinking but the one that a balding, middle-aged man sitting near the door was sipping on.

"Oo! That's our special blend," the young redhead said. "It costs a dollar more – but it has a lovely taste." Then she leaned forward and lowered her voice. "Mister Ganzeni is just about the only other person who drinks it – but he can afford to, he owns the place." She hunched up her shoulders and grinned at Derek – bandaged head and all. Mary smiled pleasantly and hoped the girl would burn herself on the expresso machine.

"Derek, why are you having coffee?" she said as the waitress flitted back into the café.

He sighed and rubbed his moustache. "I'm really not sure, but it's to do with this smell thing that seems to be taking me over."

"Is it really getting that bad?" Her concern showed on her face.

"No, it's not bad, it's…it's like I'm on this huge voyage of discovery – finding all these new things – treasures really. It was a bit confusing and scary at first – like, so much was happening in my brain.

"You mean in your nose, don't you?"

"No, it's my brain. It's like there's a sort of…pressure… as if my brain can't work fast enough to interpret all this new stuff. It was scary a couple of days ago; I thought my head was going to explode…not from pain or anything, just from figuring out stuff – and I didn't have any control over it. The closest I can explain is… You know when we were in high school and we went to Brian Cuthbertson's farewell party in year twelve?" Mary nodded. "And a whole lot of us took LSD tablets or whatever the fuck they were?"

"Yes, I remember, but I wasn't one of them."

"Yeah I know that, but I was, and it was one of the worst twenty-four hours of my life. It felt like my brain was racing along at some gigantic speed trying to make sense of all this new shit that was coming in – visual, audio, touch, the whole works; with all this weird stuff happening, completely out of the blue, all the time. Fuck, I hated it, I was totally out of control."

"So was your smell thing like that at the beginning?"

"A bit, and that's why I was worried. But it's not as racy now – more…I dunno…relaxed. And I'm sort of enjoying it. Maybe because it's not all my senses going berserk at the same time, not like they were with that fucking acid." He stopped as some people walked past. "And there's other stuff that I can feel happening now too," he whispered.

"Like what?"

"Well, there are things I just seem to know about that are to do with the smells I get, 'the aromas I believe I detect'," he said in a affected tone, mimicking Doctor Barrington – who still maintained Derek was hallucinating. Mary allowed herself to grin. "Like with the period thing with the nurses," he went on. "I knew straight away what that smell was…what it meant. It's as though I already had the smell and its meaning stored away somewhere in my brain – like maybe I'd learned it ages ago without actually knowing it at the time, and never being able to use it."

"Until now," Mary said.

"Until now," he confirmed. "Then there are other smells – 'aromas' (he did the voice thing again) – that I can't link to anything straight away. There's been a couple of instances when I've been able to work out what they mean…" He stopped as the waitress approached and then put down their coffees. As she bent forward, the pendant on her necklace swung out from her open blouse. "That's an interesting pendant," he said while she straightened up, having cast a flirtatious grin in his direction. "What's it made of?"

The girl glanced at Mary and then squatted on her haunches next to Derek, holding out the object on the end of the silver chain. "It's from Tonga," she said, made from the tooth of a sperm whale."

Mary was sure that the girl had put an ever-so-subtle emphasis on the word 'sperm', and fleetingly wondered whether it was possible to kill someone with a teaspoon.

Derek took hold of the pendant – it was flat and a few millimetres thick, and more or less shaped like a triangle with rounded ends; the image of a palm tree and water and a crescent moon were finely burnt into the surface. "It's called 'scrumshaw'," the girl said as she hung onto the table with her other hand, forcing out her chest at the same time.

"Scrimshaw," Mary said without smiling.

The waitress gave her a disdainful glance. "Whatever," she replied. "My ex-boyfriend gave it to me last year."

"Very nice," Derek said, blinking and sitting back in his chair, his nostrils visibly flaring. The girl placed the pendant back into her blouse, effortlessly stood up, and walked back into the café. "There's a perfect example of what I was just talking about," he said to Mary.

"How do you mean?" she replied, trying to dismiss her annoyance.

"See, that smell coming from her pendant…couldn't you detect it?"

Mary scrunched up her mouth. "No, but then I didn't have my nose hovering just above her cleavage like you." She was immediately sorry for the remark, sure that Derek had been quite innocent of any furtive behaviour. As it was, he paid no attention to her sarcasm.

"Anyway, I could detect a new and different sort of smell coming from that girl's open shirt – apart from all the other smells coming from her that I already sort of understood." Mary bit her top lip and nodded. "I couldn't for the life of me understand what this strange odour meant – it was like a mix of the ocean and of fire…with just a hint of other things too. When she said it was whale ivory, and I could see those tiny burnt images, well…it made sense. And from now on I'll always be able to identify that smell. If she hadn't shown me the pendant then I would never have understood what was going on." He sipped from his cup. "And that's what's happening most of the time with me at the moment," he added. "Not understanding what I'm detecting, I mean."

Mary couldn't help herself. Her eyes narrowed. "And what about her 'other' odours?" she said, "…I mean Little

Miss Tart-in-your-face...what could you detect there?"

Derek raised his eyebrows. "Not a lot," he replied.

"Oh, come on Derek, your nostrils flared out like elephant's ears when she was squatting next to you – you obviously got a blast of something. You don't have to have a heightened sense of smell to know what was going on, her behaviour said it all – the little flirt was just about slipping on the concrete. Come on, be honest with me, she must have smelled to you like she was on heat."

Derek frowned and then leaned forward and spoke quietly. "Actually, there's a lot of sadness associated with the odours coming from that girl and, for your information, she didn't smell at all fertile – not like the nurse the other night. What struck me like a hammer blow when she was next to me wasn't exactly *her* odour. It was someone else's – all over her, and...elsewhere." He sat back in his chair and looked at the café entrance. Mary's forehead wrinkled as she tried to figure out what her husband was going on about. "He likes fine coffee and young waitresses it would seem," he said, pointing with his chin at the café's owner, "and I'm fairly sure he's not a very nice person," he added as he pushed himself away from the table.

Even before they were halfway up the track, it was obvious to Mary that her husband was again being overwhelmed. On at least three other occasions during their journey home from Trelborough she had noticed a similar reaction: sitting back in his seat, eyes widening, nostrils flaring; then, after a minute or so, his shoulders would slump, he'd blink, and he'd snort out air through his nose – as if cleansing it of the molecules that had caused his brain to work overtime. Now, almost home, it was happening again.

"Are you okay?" she asked, not for the first time today.

Derek snorted and then lifted his head and sniffed in more air. "Amazing," was all he could manage to get out, his fascination with what he was detecting being plain. There was no time for discussion; no time for explanation. Then, just before the car entered the garage, he suddenly opened the passenger door. "Stop! Stop!" he called without even looking at her.

Mary hit the brake pedal and they both jerked forward. A second or two later Derek was running down the slope on the western side of the track, away from the house. Mary didn't bother to park the car – just left it where it was, and attempted to follow him. However, he'd already disappeared into the masses of spindly gums and long grass that populated this side of their property. She followed the trail he'd made but still couldn't see him, and was about to call out when she caught a glimpse of him kneeling behind a large boulder. It was near the bank of the creek that meandered along this part of their block – sometimes a swirling torrent if there'd been continual rain up in the hills but now no more than a trickle, with occasional large pools. He was still some way off but she could see that he was signalling her to be quiet and to lower her body.

"Shhh," he whispered, as she ran up, an index finger touching his lips. Mary frowned. It was difficult enough hurrying through this terrain while crouching, she didn't need to be shushed. "Look," he said softly, pointing to a small clearing about sixty metres away on the other side of the creek. She peeked over the boulder. It took a moment for her eyes to see into the shadows but when they did, her jaw dropped in surprise. There on the pebbled bank, beneath the sunlight-blocking branches of a large poinsettia, were two creatures: a dingo, and a goanna. The dingo was of mature size, its white-tipped tail flouncing about as the animal stepped backwards and forwards in front of its adversary – urgently, but with appropriate caution. The two-metre long goanna, on the other hand, stood its ground, following the motion of the dingo with only slight movements of its head and neck. Both humans watched, transfixed, as the tan-coated canine, with its to-and-fro motion, tried to catch the reptile off-guard. Even though they were some way off, Mary and Derek could hear the distinctive high-pitched 'singing' of the dingo and the loud, throaty hissing of its would-be prey.

Suddenly, the dingo lunged at the goanna, seeming to go for its neck. It was then that the goanna's latent swiftness came to the fore. In a flash of movement it countered the attack, first by sinking its own razor-sharp teeth into its opponent's snout, and then – as the dingo let out a yelp and backed off – by running towards the poinsettia and disappearing up its trunk at an astonishing speed. The dingo, having quickly recovered from the surprise nip, ran to the base of the tree and circled it several times, all the while looking up into the branches. It then sat down, still looking skyward, clearly having spied the creature that it now intended to keep under siege. Derek turned to his wife.

"He'll get tired of waiting and go back to his den after a while," he whispered. "The goanna'll live to fight another day. Come on, let's go." He turned to leave.

"Wait a minute, you," Mary said trying to keep her voice low but still emphatic. "Why did you come running down here in the first place?" She sat down on the ground with her back against the boulder – she had no intention of moving.

Derek turned back and joined her on the ground. "I'm sorry Sweetie," he said. "I just knew that there was a dingo – a male – and…I thought it was a snake; that they were close together, maybe fighting."

"Jesus, you could smell that?"

Derek paused for a moment, stroking his chin and looking to one side. "Well…yeah," he said, "I suppose I could."

Mary slowly shook her head. "I can understand

your heightened ability to detect aromas and odours and whatever – because of some freakish thing happening to your brain as a result of the accident – but I'm having trouble seeing how you can know..."

Derek interrupted her. "It's like I said before, I think it's stored memories – smell memories – that I haven't even been aware of."

"But where would've you known about dingo smells… and the odour of snakes or goannas?"

He leaned back next to her. "Remember that private zoo near the Sunshine Coast we went to a couple of years ago?"

"Yes."

"In one section there some dingoes – at one end of the enclosure there was a bitch lying down with four or five pups hanging off her teats, and at the other end there was a big male. And later in the morning we watched that guy handling all those snakes in the reptile display area. There was that huge python that frightened the shit out of little Harry."

"You mean it's smells from that visit, smells that you weren't aware of at the time, that you're brain is now remembering and linking to?"

"Well, all I know is that while we were driving up the track, I caught these odours, and at the same time I suddenly recalled images, you know, actual visual images, of that trip – the male dingo, the python…"

"But it wasn't a python we just saw, it was a goanna, so what's going on there?"

Derek sighed. "Geez, I dunno – there were a couple of goannas in the reptile section of that zoo…maybe I was smelling the goannas while I was looking at the python…"

"And you got them mixed up."

"Yeah, I got 'em mixed up."

Mary put her arm around her husband. "You poor old thing," she said. "That's probably going to happen quite a bit over the next few days, I expect."

He looked at her and smiled, deciding not to mention anything of his concern about how long this new 'ability' of his was going to last – and if it did persist, whether it would turn out to be an affliction or a blessing. He stood up and peered over the boulder; Mary did the same. The dingo was still sitting under the tree, oblivious to their presence. "Lucky we're upwind," Mary whispered. "Come on, let's go." She took Derek's hand and, hunched over, they crept away.

"You know how we used to fantasize about one day owning a pub?" Derek said in a low voice once they were some distance away. Mary nodded. "Well what do you think of 'The Dog and Lizard' as a name?" They took a few more steps. "You know, dingo, goanna – dog, lizard. Woddaya think?"

"Remind me to loosen your bandage when we get to the house," she replied.

In the afternoon, Mary left to collect Harry from school, and to do a little shopping in Yuragan. Derek was sitting in front of the television set watching a game show. Mary had told him he had to relax and to not do anything even remotely related to work; 'The boating world can wait until next Monday for you to start,' she had said. He looked at the game show host and the pretty girl next to him. They were having some inane conversation about her recent holiday. Rifkin was curled up in his basket – ostensibly asleep – but he promptly raised his head as Derek got up from the couch and turned off the TV. "Come on Rifkin," he said. "Any more of this bullshit and my brain'll turn into marshmallow."

He opened the flyscreen door at the end of the lounge room and stepped onto the veranda that ran around three of the house's four sides. First, he leaned on the railing and gazed out over the bushland that surrounded his and Mary's small property – he stared in the direction of the creek, where the dingo and goanna encounter had taken place earlier; he thought he could just make out the top of the poinsettia where the big lizard had found refuge. Suddenly he felt a wave of aromas sweep over all his other perceptions of the world, almost drowning them into insignificance. He straightened up and held onto one of the vertical posts – the pressure from the accompanying mental processing almost making him dizzy. It was strange; he wasn't aware of what was actually going on in his head during these moments, but he knew there was definitely something big happening up there. It was like when he once visited a part of the Snowy Mountains hydroelectric scheme when he was a kid. He and his schoolmates had started to walk over what seemed to be just an ordinary field, with a crop – tobacco, he thought – growing in it. But as they crossed that field, he'd known there was something unusual going on, something just on the edge of his perception; a slight vibration in the ground perhaps, or a low, barely-audible rumbling. A lot of the kids had felt it, and some had even become scared. It was only later, when they'd gone down the long, spiralling stairwell in the bunker-like building at the end of the field, that they understood what they'd felt – that under the field there was a vast powerplant producing zillions of watts of electricity, with megalitres of water blasting through the turbine housings every minute, and men in white overalls and wearing earmuffs walking around checking instruments and various subsystems. If he and the other kids hadn't seen what was going on, if they'd just walked over the field, the only impression they would've been left with was that something powerful but totally unknowable was going on beneath them. Well, what was happening in his head at these times was sort of like that…but…

Derek's brief reminiscence dissolved as he noticed a particular odour that stood out from the rest. They were all of immense interest, yet he chose to ignore most of them – as best he could. However, this one for some reason, had special appeal. He looked down at Rifkin who had followed him out onto the veranda. The dog seemed to have noticed the same smell – his ears were pricked up and his head was sticking out through the rails, pointing in the direction that Derek knew the smell was coming from. Suddenly, Rifkin pulled his head back and looked up at his master. "Pussycat!" Derek said. Rifkin gave a subdued yelp and immediately scrambled to the end of the veranda and down the stairs. Derek was close behind him, not analysing, not deliberating, not thinking about anything really – the feline smell was all that was important; it was strong and the animal was close, and this chase was going to be...fun.

Chapter 3

Mary was frowning – it was the one that somehow managed to convey anger, disbelief, and pleading all at the same time. Or was it the smell she was exuding? No, it was her face, the frown, he'd seen it heaps of times before. But the smell…

"Shit, Derek," she said, slamming the fridge door so hard that a variety of magnetic cards fell to the floor. "You told me that you'd stay home until Monday – that's three days away, the least time the doctor said you should take it easy and not work."

"I know what I told you," he replied, "But I think it's important that I get back to work as soon as I can."

"Why? Why is it so necessary for you to put your recovery in jeopardy?"

He always felt a little uncomfortable when she used uncommon words – like 'jeopardy'. Sometimes he had no idea what they meant, but usually it was just a case of being a tiny bit uncertain, or simply not practiced in their use. He bent down and picked up the floppy little magnets from the floor. 'Jeopardy', it was a funny word; he remembered how he'd looked at it in a newspaper just a while back and realized that it was very close to 'leopard'. Suddenly, he thought about the cat chase with Rifkin the previous day; how they'd pounded through the scrub together after the terrified creature – its fear in his nostrils – with the dog barking and him yelling. Of course, it got away, disappearing into the nearby state forest – probably up a tree, like the goanna. By luck or design, the cat – almost certainly ferrel – had stayed downwind of its two pursuers, and they both had difficulty keeping up with its scent once they got into the thick bush. Besides, Derek wasn't used to running at such speed, and eventually he'd had to stop, dropping to his knees amongst the ferns. As he'd knelt there, with his heart pounding and his chest heaving, and the scent fading, he'd realized that if they'd caught the cat, then he would've torn it apart without a second thought – without any thought at all. And he'd suddenly been appalled. Mary knew nothing of the chase…or of his concern. No, staying at home alone again, just now, might not be a good idea.

He looked at the top magnet; it was for Lawrie Wellington's steam cleaning service. Before sticking it back on the fridge, he held it up to Mary. "Do you think we need our carpets cleaned?" he said, trying to smile.

"Oh piss off Derek," Mary replied. "If you want to

kill yourself by going back to work the day after you were released from hospital then go ahead." She glared at him, and then her face reddened and her eyes became watery. "Why are you doing this?" she said in a now-quavering voice.

Derek knew that more than words were needed at this moment. He walked up to her and placed his arms around her shoulders, and held her close.

"Would it be so hard to just stay home and rest?" she said while he stroked her short, brown hair.

He gently separated himself from the embrace and looked into her tear-filled eyes. "Look, I promise I'll take it just as easy down at the yacht club as I would if I were here. Jono can do all the work; I'll just sit and supervise. Please believe me when I say it'll be better for me if I go to work."

Mary wiped her eyes on her bare arm. She could sense her husband's resolve, and knew this was not an argument she was going to win. "Promise you'll not do anything active?" He nodded. "And that you'll get Jono to drive you home if you feel the least bit tired or dizzy or anything else that makes you uncomfortable?"

He nodded again and then said, "Does that include that bloody horrible music that Jono sometimes plays on the van's CD-player?"

She slapped his chest, and snorted out a laugh. She then looked into his eyes and held his gaze, as if to emphasize what she was about to say. "Be careful then, Derek," she said. "Just be careful."

The solemness of the moment was broken by Harry who walked in from the lounge room holding a feather. "Hey, Daddy," he said. "I've got a good idea for you. But you have to promise to do what I say."

It was the first time Derek had sat on the passenger side of the van for ages – not since he'd dislocated his shoulder playing soccer in that fund-raising competition a few years ago. "Jesus, this seat is a bit hard isn't it?" he said to Jono who was driving. And then, looking out from the side window, "You're a bit close to the fucking edge here mate – get over to the middle more."

Jono pulled on the wheel slightly and then centred it again. They were now on the straight section of road next to Kempsey Beach – palm trees, sand, and ocean. The apprentice glanced across at his boss, and grinned. "It really does look good," he said, referring back to an observation he'd made when first arriving at the workshop in the morning. Derek remained silent. "I mean, the brown in the feather is just nicely set off by the white bandage – very...chiefly looking."

"Go fuck yourself," Derek said without turning.

Later, in the boatyard, Jono was standing next to an old, plywood-hulled motor cruiser – he had an electric jigsaw in his hand. Derek was nearby, sitting on the unfolded director's chair that Mary had insisted he take with him. "Okay, the square you've drawn around the hole looks fine. Now all you have to do is cut it out and…"

"I've only done this about fifty times before, you know," his apprentice answered just before pressing the trigger and beginning the cut – the resulting noise making further conversation impossible.

Derek leaned back into the chair's canvas, and smiled. Jono was such a different fella now compared to when he'd started. Four years ago you wouldn't get a boo out of him – certainly no answering back. He'd been a real timid kid. But by geez he learned quick…and it was obvious that he loved the work. Still does. And the shyness? Shit, that just seemed to erode away like antifouling as he got more confident about what he was doing – both in his job and in his personal life. Finally standing up to that fucking piss-head of a father had sorted out a lot of things for him too. No, Jono was all right, and he still knew when to keep his mouth closed. Usually, anyhow.

This reflective interlude promptly ceased when Derek suddenly became aware of a particular odour. The scents of the kauri pine and resorcinol glue being blasted out with the sawdust that Jono was creating were strong, but there was that other smell again, the one that had been coming from Jono himself all morning – a girl smell, warm and voluptuous and wet. He closed his eyes and saw young Wendy Butler – Jono's new true-love. The same thing had happened on the way to the yacht club – in the van. He'd been able to dismiss the thoughts and images then, but for some reason it was harder now – even though the scent was much weaker. It was as though the subtlety of the odour, the very fact that it was only barely detectable, made it more tantalizing, more powerful. He opened his eyes. The visual image of the Butler girl disappeared, but he still felt her presence, his brain conjuring her up in other ways that he couldn't quite understand. And then he became aware of his erection, so big that it hurt. He stood up and walked along the path to the back of the clubhouse – to where there was a stainless steel sink that yard workers could use for washing off grime and dust. Jesus, Wendy Butler was just a kid…and how did he know it was really her that he was smelling? Had his mind just taken an unknown female scent and linked it to pictures of Wendy because he knew that she was Jono's girlfriend? Or was it one of the many scents that he genuinely recognized from past exposure – despite being oblivious to their presence at the time? Asking Jono if he'd been with Wendy this morning might help resolve the issue but at the moment he just wanted to get her out of his mind. That's what the rational part of him was saying at least – the part that included moral attitudes and concerns about appropriate behaviour. A more basic part of him – the part that seemed to be almost directly linked to his new ability – just wanted him to find Wendy Butler, and to root her.

And this scared the shit out of him.

He turned on the tap and cupped some cold water over his face, trying not to wet the bandage that angled down from his forehead to the back of his skull. As he fought to dismiss all impressions of the young woman from his mind – by thinking about something mundane and practical, like how to best install the new anchor winch on that big cruiser after lunch – someone spoke.

"G'day, mate; don't you look a bloody mess?" Derek lifted his head. The voice belonged to Fergus O'Brien, a giant of a man in his early fifties. He was the caretaker of the yacht club. He'd been away at the time of Derek's accident but, of course, he knew all the details – as did half the population of Yuragan by now.

Derek forced a smile. "Not as much as I did a few days ago," he said.

The big man had also been smiling but now his brow furrowed. "Is that a feather stickin' out of the bandage?"

"Yes, Fergus, it's a feather." Derek waited for the inevitable next question, or a smart-arse observation, but neither came.

"Ya know, Slinky was down 'ere early this mornin'. He said you weren't comin' back until Mond'y. It's gunna be a while before he gets over havin' knocked you off that trestle, ya know."

"Yeah, well I certainly won't be anywhere near him when he's backing his boat in the future," Derek replied, wiping some water from his chin.

"The committee's already banned him from using the club tractor, ya know," Fergus replied. "They had an emergency meeting the night after your accident. Yours was the second he'd caused with the tractor this month – old bugger's losin' his coordination. They made him promise he'd always get someone else t'do his towin' in the yard from now on – otherwise they were gunna ban his boat from bein' 'ere."

"Oh, there was no need to threaten him with that," Derek replied, annoyed. "Slinky knows he's getting old; he'd understand if he was asked – they didn't have to threaten him." He remembered that his father and Slinky Robinson had fought in the Korean War together – remembered the story of how they'd got drunk with a bunch of other Yuragan boys the night before they all enlisted; remembered his father telling him how some had never returned. "He came to see me in the hospital, you know – the next day," Derek said, recalling how distraught and apologetic the old man had been; and that Mary had taken him to the cafeteria to calm him down with a cup of tea. "Fucking committee," he said quietly.

The big man paused while looking at Derek's face, and then altered the direction of the conversation. "So howaya feelin'?", he said.

Derek liked Fergus – he was another local boy, of which there weren't too many left these days. Fergus was older, but they'd known each other since primary school. Derek still remembered that day long ago when he'd been in grade five, and Fergus had taken care of the school bully – a new kid – who had been making his life a misery. You don't forget things like that. He was about to respond to the big fella's question when an aroma seemed to envelop him.

"Are you brewing peppermint tea?" he asked.

Fergus made a clicking sound in his mouth, and looked both embarrassed and surprised. "Bloody hell," he said. "How'd ya know that?" And before Derek could answer, he added, "The boss," (referring to his wife, Marge), "says I have to have it because of my sore gut – s'posed to be good for it."

Derek smiled. "Well I really like the stuff," he said. "And Marge is right, it's helped my insides when they've been movin' like a bag of tiger snakes. Sort of calms things down."

Fergus looked relieved. He'd been ribbed enough about his peppermint tea by the real-men of the club. "Do ya want some, then?" he asked.

"Yeah, that'd be good," Derek replied.

They walked up the stairs that would take them into the main room of the clubhouse from which they could enter the small kitchen. Halfway up, Fergus stopped and turned around. "You didn't tell me how ya knew what I was brewin' – it's way over in the bloody kitchen. I can't smell anythin' from here."

Derek grinned, there were other smells vying for his attention now besides the peppermint. "Keep going," he said, indicating with a push of his chin, "I'll tell you all about it – but only if you promise to keep it under your hat."

"A secret?" Fergus said as he continued the climb.

"Yeah, a secret," the single-feathered boatbuilder replied.

Fergus wasn't the brightest bulb in the box, but everyone who knew him appreciated having him around. He was one of those people you occasionally come across who seem to have been dealt out a large serve of innate goodness when they were little – and then, unlike most others, had managed to keep it all the way into adulthood. You could talk to Big F, as some of the locals teasingly called him, about almost anything of a personal nature. He'd never say a lot, mainly just listen. But when he did speak, it made sense, and you'd usually go away feeling better about yourself, or with the resolve to make things better. His wisdom always seemed simple at first; sort of homespun and uncomplicated. But then when you thought about it, you often got the feeling that his words were maybe carrying something deeper and more involved. Like some of those paintings you see. They appear fairly straightforward when you first look at them, but then, on closer examination, they have all these little details of other things that are going on. Derek once told his wife that if the world was going to end and he was given the opportunity to choose twenty people to take with him to another planet, then Fergus would be one of his choices. Mary had understood immediately (after checking that she and the kids were also on the list – and at the top).

"So what else can ya smell…like right now, I mean?" Fergus said.

Derek didn't answer for a few seconds; just sat at the table with his eyes closed, consciously examining the odours that were currently streaming over him, around him, through him. Even though he'd only had this heightened detection ability for a few days, he could already consciously bring separate parts of the stream out of the swirling background for a closer study. It was a bit like focusing your eyes on one particular object in a crowded visual scene – and then repeating the process with other objects. "Let's see," he said. "I know someone had eggs and fried tomato on toast for breakfast here today – and…mustard, or something like that."

Fergus sat back in his chair. "What about bacon?"

Derek didn't hesitate. "No, there was definitely no bacon,"

The big man slowly shook his head. "That's bloody amazing. There was a big kerfuffle here this mornin' with Barry Oldridge and the crew from that ketch down on the pontoon. You know how Barry comes here almost every day now for breakfast – ever since his old lady pissed him off. Anyway, he was here this mornin' and he reckoned someone'd pinched his bacon from the fridge. Ya should'a seen him, he was wild; stompin' around and cursin' – effin' this and effin' that – and suggestin' that these visitors had taken it. At one point I thought this young fella was gunna give him a smack – I wouldn'ave blamed him, either. But I managed to calm both of 'em down, and the ketch people ended up sharing their breakfast with Barry – eggs and fried tomato…and a sprinkling of mustard seeds – they made a big thing about the seeds." He rested his chin at the top of his clasped hands, and stared from across the table. "Geez, Derek, you've really got somethin' there," he said. "What else?"

"Well, you had Woofa in here today, didn't ya?" The words had only just left his mouth when Derek regretted saying them. He knew it was against the yacht club's rules to have dogs inside the building, but he hadn't meant the sentence to come out like an accusation.

"Yeah, well, Woofa's a mate, and there's some rules ya don't mind breakin' if it's for a mate. But ya choose ya times."

Derek felt like a dickhead. "Oh, look, sorry Fergus, I wasn't having a go at you. You could have the whole fuckin' kennel club in here and I wouldn't care." He looked at his old school friend. He didn't say anything, but he could now actually *smell* the man's resolve. He knew what it was, but he had no idea of how to explain it. Eggs and tomato and mustard and dogs were okay, but resolve? stubbornness? How do you describe those smells? Maybe you don't…because maybe they're not really there… He ran his hand over the unbandaged top part of his head, and sighed.

"You sure got a gift given to ya when ya fell off that trestle," Fergus said. "I gave Woofa a bath last night. I thought he ended up smellin' more like Velvet soap than a dog. Amazin'." There was silence for a short while – not uncomfortable – and then he spoke again. "But ya worried about it aren't ya?"

Derek took a sip of his now barely-warm peppermint tea, and nodded. He knew he could trust Fergus, and was sure that sharing his concerns – his fears – about the times when the smells take over, might lead to some useful insights. He was wondering how to begin his explanation when Jono burst into the room – safety glasses up on his forehead, and a white dust mask hanging under his chin.

"Sorry fellas, I don't want to interrupt," he said to the seated pair, and then turned to Derek, "But I think you might want to see something, boss," indicating that this was a business 'something', not for Fergus or anyone else.

The big man stayed seated while Derek got up and walked to the doorway where his apprentice was standing.

"What's going on?" he asked quietly.

Jono stepped out of the room and onto the stairway landing. Derek followed. "I was fitting the patch on the inside of the old cruiser when I slipped. I had a screw driver in my hand, and it went through a nearby stringer."

"Oh, fuck," Derek said. "Dry rot?"

"Yep, and not just in that stringer – there's frames, panels, even bits of the hull."

Derek twisted his mouth. The boat's owner didn't appear to have much money – he'd probably not be able to afford any extensive professional repairs, but they'd have to tell him the bad news. Fucking old plywood boats. He stuck his head back into the room, the end of his feather bending in the cross breeze. Fergus was still sitting at the table. "I'll have to go, Fergus," he called. "Something's come up." He followed Jono down the stairs, pissed off that he hadn't pinpointed the dry rot himself. He'd smelled it as soon as they'd arrived in the boat yard, but it was all over the place. He just hadn't associated it with the old vessel that Jono had been working on. Fuck! What an idiot. At the bottom of the stairs he stopped – Jono was still walking ahead. He'd really wanted to talk to Fergus about the darker side of what was happening to him. But he could probably do that later. He hoped so – especially now that he'd again caught that tantalizing whiff of Wendy Butler.

When they arrived home the sun was just setting. Jono left almost immediately, his clapped out Holden grunting and roaring it's way down the track. Derek stood for a minute and admired the colour display in the western sky. In winter, and from where he was standing, the hill at the back of Mendelson's farm would force a premature sunset, and there would never be much to look at. But by early September the mechanics of the solar system had done their thing and you could see the sun dropping below the far-off horizon to the left of the hill. This meant that the Sadler place received even more daylight in the warmer months, and there was the added benefit of spectacular light shows in the sky – not every evening, mind, but fairly often. Derek had always had a particular liking for the pinks, especially when they were set against the darkening blues higher in the sky – sometimes these merged to produce a band of purple, although Mary always said it was just his imagination. He sighed through his nose. Of course, the sun's disappearance also heralded the coming of the scents of the night. To him, now, this shift was just as noticeable as the visual changes. For the moment, though, he was able to suppress his keen osmatic awareness of the surroundings, and just take in the beauty afforded him by his eyes. But those scents, some of them were just so beguiling…

Suddenly something cold touched his hand. "What the f…" He looked down and saw Rifkin standing beside him, and then turned as a poorly-suppressed giggle filled his ears. Mary and Harry and Tim – his whole family – were standing behind him.

Harry took his hand from his mouth and a stream of gurgling laughs shot out as he ran to his father. Derek swept up the six year-old in his powerful arms. "Geez, you guys really snuck up on me didn't ya?" he said with a smile. He noticed that Mary was also smiling. Tim, on the other hand, looked uncomfortable – even glancing away when Derek's eyes met his.

"You didn't know we were here, did you Daddy?" Harry said, still excited by the success of their sneak-up.

"I certainly didn't, young fella," his father replied while walking up to the other two, accompanied by Rifkin.

"We all thought it would be nice to give you a special greeting when you got home today," Mary said, reaching out and taking his spare hand, "Especially since you shouldn't have gone to work in the first place.

He gave a little jump of his eyebrows – in an 'oh, well' gesture – and then turned to Tim. The teenager spoke first.

"I didn't know about your accident until I got home this afternoon," he said, showing little emotion.

"No, well, your mother and I didn't want to spoil your camp…and you were six hundred kilometres away – not just down the road. Anyway, it wasn't as though I was gunna die or anything…"

While Derek waited for more words to come, Tim reached out and, with head down, offered him what looked like a piece of coloured paper. Mary took Harry so her husband could more easily examine the offering. Rather than paper, Derek saw that it was a folded card that appeared to have been cut from a Manila folder. On the front was a black-line border framing the words 'FOR DAD', in green and yellow. Inside the card was written 'Get Well Soon' in big, multicoloured letters, and underneath, in a smaller font and in parentheses, 'I really don't want mum to teach me to drive'. It was simply signed 'Tim'. Derek stared down at the card. He felt his throat tightening and the hint of a tear forming in each eye. He then stepped forward and enclosed his older son in his arms. "Thanks Tim," he said softly into the lad's ear. He didn't feel any reciprocal hug from his boy – it'd been an awful long time since they'd actually touched each other at all – but when he dropped his arms and stepped back, he noticed that Tim now allowed himself to look into his eyes, and to grin – even if only for a moment.

"Did it without any prompting from me," Mary whispered as they all climbed the stairs to the house. Derek felt happy – the feeling overrode all those that his sense of smell was bringing forth. And he was sure he could detect the smell of happiness coming from his family members – each with its own special signature. But these he didn't mind dwelling on – they added to his own uplifted state.

"And did you wear my feather all day like you promised?" Harry said as they stepped onto the landing.

Derek laughed – for the first time in weeks – a good belly laugh. "Yes," he said. "All day long."

A faint glow remained in the sky when he walked out onto the side veranda. He'd spent longer than usual in the shower, but the warm water on his back had alleviated the pain in his muscles – nothing serious, but still sore as a result of his fall. He was a lot wearier than he'd anticipated – crawling around that plywood boat had intensified a few aches that he'd hardly been aware of. As he lowered himself into his favourite chair – canvas and cushions and wide, wooden armrests – he grunted; maybe he should've stopped work earlier. From the gully he could smell what he thought were echidnas – probably scratching in the ground and amongst the leaf litter for grubs and other tasty morsels. Rifkin had bailed one up when he was still growing, just a dog teenager, but he'd yelped like a little puppy when he'd got one of those spines in his nose; every living creature within a kilometre radius must have heard him. He'd stayed well clear of echidnas ever since.

Derek concentrated. He could also sense a wombat. It was heading in the same direction – working its way down to the creek from the farthest slope, probably having just emerged from its burrow. And there were birds and reptiles and other little creatures that he could detect – the evening taking on a whole new olfactory perspective as the night hunters and foragers began to stir: mopokes and geckos and bandicoots and possums. Of course, there were also the plant smells that seemed to become more prominent as darkness descended. Most he couldn't identify, but he knew a few: the subtle scents of the big tallowwoods and bunya pines up in the state forest, and the stronger smells coming from the tea-trees and mangroves closer to the coast. The most beautiful, though, was the scent of the native frangipani. Not the imported variety – that was in abundance too but the scent was overbearing and sickly sweet. The native variety, however, had a scent that was… exquisite. There were also the rocks: the basalts and the schist; and the water in the creek: that which flowed, and that which was still. Derek closed his eyes and shifted his attention to these other aromas, but the process was suddenly interrupted by a new, powerful smell, one that he immediately recognized.

"Here's a beer for you…Dad."

Derek blinked. Tim was standing beside him holding a Crown Lager and a glass. This was a bit of a treat for Derek. He didn't drink much anymore – not like in his younger days – but when he did have the occasional stubbie, it was Crown that he preferred. The trouble was, though, it was so bloody expensive. He took the bottle and glass – Mary had told him a long time ago that if he was going to drink expensive beer then he should do it from a glass – and watched his son amble away. Was it sadness that he was catching a whiff of? "Hey, Tim," he said, "Why don't you come and sit with me for a while?"

The boy stopped and turned, indecision on his face. "Well, I've…" He paused.

"Come on," Derek beckoned with his bottle hand and in so doing splashed some beer over the groin area of his shorts. He looked down. "Oh, fuck, look! I look like I've pissed meself." They both laughed.

"I'll get you a cloth," Tim said.

"No, bugger it. It's only a tiny patch. Come and sit with me. I'll share this stubby with you."

He saw the surprise on Tim's face – he'd never before offered his son alcohol, uncertain about what age the boy should be when such offers might be made, and not even sure if it was right for parents to introduce the stuff to their kids at all. But there it was, on the table, offered without any forethought or planning. Derek felt the surprise on his own face.

Tim walked back to his father and sat in the adjacent chair. Derek poured half the beer into the glass and gave the stubbie to his son. "Prost," he said as they clinked containers.

Tim smiled. "Prost," he said.

"Now, tell me about the camp – start with getting off the bus – what was your first impression." Then, as an immediate afterthought, he added, "And before I forget, later on, let's organize these driving lessons that I'll be giving you."

Tim was still smiling, something Derek hadn't seen him maintain for a long time.

"Well, as soon as we arrived, this big ranger-type guy comes up to us and says…"

When Mary came in from the bathroom, Derek was still awake – wide awake. This not only surprised her but also him. He'd been weary when he first got home but now he was still hyped up from the happenings of the evening. He felt an almost triumphant sort of happiness as a result of his long chat with Tim. God! They'd laughed and joked and enjoyed each other's company just like the old days before the kid's hormones had kicked in – and, Derek suspected, before he himself had become so obsessed with his work that he'd forgotten how to be a good father. He watched Mary lift the blanket. *Or a good husband*, he thought.

"I know I've already said it half a dozen times, but geez that meal was good," he said as he touched her arm. "That sauce on the lamb was just so delicious; I can still taste it."

She stopped adjusting her pillows just long enough to give him a brief look of enticement – like a latter-day

Mona Lisa – and then reached for the book on her bedside table. "Yes, well I was fairly happy with how it turned out," she said.

She didn't look at Derek when she spoke – just opened up her book – but he was sure she was deliberately trying to be nonchalant. He reached this conclusion not only as a result of years of observing his wife's behaviour, but also because of a scent that he was now aware of – one of the overwhelming kind. Hers. It wasn't just her usual smell, although that had different minor…'flavours'…being added and subtracted all the time – like everybody else's. No, this was an addition that mixed with her signature smell to produce something that practically took his breath away. And he was pretty sure where most of it was coming from.

He looked at his wife. She was so beautiful. Sitting there propped up against the bed head reading a book, the cut of her short, brown hair showing off the smoothness of her slender neck, and the pink in her light-weight night dress contrasting with the tan of her arms and chest. And her breasts, so full and alluring; with her nipples pushing through the flimsy fabric, announcing their existence – proudly – even though covered from view. He took a deep breath. Her scent – that scent – was even more intrusive. Luscious and inviting. A similar awareness had caused him much concern earlier in the day – but he didn't want to revisit those thoughts and desires – couldn't really, thank God. But this was different, this was his wife. He'd felt strong desire for her before, of course, but not like this – he was now just totally awash with it, just wanting to fuck her for all of eternity, hard and repeatedly. He gently ran his fingers down her cheek and neck, and onto the top of her breast, and then circled the protruding nipple.

Mary put the book on her lap. "My goodness," she said. "What's got into you?"

"Mmmm," he whispered as he mouthed her ear. "I think you might be asking that question about yourself soon." He pressed himself against her.

"Oooh," she replied slowly. "I see what you mean."

Later, much later than ever before, Mary lay with her head on Derek's chest. The night wasn't particularly warm but both were still sweating; exhausted and sweating; and feeling exulted and relaxed and, in Mary's case, a little mystified about what had just happened during the last hour.

"My God, Derek," she said, reaching down and twirling the pubic hair just below his navel. "If that's what rosemary and honey sauce does to you then I think we might be having it fairly often." She groaned and stretched her palm across his stomach.

He chuckled, and then sighed; drained of energy but completely content. Mary, however, lifted herself from his chest and leaned on one of her elbows, surveying his face, her curiosity clearly piqued. "Really, though, what brought all that on?" she said. "I don't believe for a minute it was anything you ate." She flopped onto her back, next to him, and pulled her knees up to her chest – making another delectable groan. "I mean, I'm not complaining," she said as she straightened her legs and then rolled over and kissed him on the cheek. "It's just that I can't remember you ever being so…so…"

"What, so *wild*, do you mean," he said, suddenly feeling a tiny arrow of guilt penetrate his blissful state.

"Wild was just part of it," she replied, closing her eyes. "But…*attentive* too." She looked across at him, her chin almost touching his shoulder. "Quite wonderful, really."

Derek turned to her, glad that she had just dismissed his concern about perhaps being too rough. "Do you want to know what it was?" he said, feeling his body and mind descending from the plateau of contentment, down towards normalcy.

Mary nodded. "Uh huh."

He leaned back. "It's to do with this," he said, pointing to his bandaged head.

She frowned. "How do you mean?"

"Well…" Derek hesitated for a moment, trying to find the right words. "Well, one of the things I'm finding with this enhanced smell ability…"

"*Hyperosmia*," Mary interrupted. "I looked it up on the Web. Sorry."

"Yeah, well, whatever it is, one of the effects is that there are certain smells that just…just take me over. It's not exactly the smells themselves…but the way they trigger all these different thoughts and images and…desires. I've had to use all my thinking power to stop from just…you know…running with the flow. It frightens the shit out of me, really. I'm scared I'll let myself go when it's…you know…totally inappropriate." He took a deep breath, and saw the concern on his wife's face. "I mean, like, yesterday while you were picking up Harry from school, I went running off into the bush with Rifkin – chasing a fucking cat. I didn't even think about what I was doing until I just couldn't run any more. I mean, the scent just made me do it without any mulling over or decision making or anything."

"But you're starting to control that sort of effect, right?" Mary asked.

"Yeah; well, I think so. But it's only happened a few times in such a powerful way." He decided not to say anything about earlier in the day.

"And what just happened here," Mary said. "How was that related to these overwhelming odours?" She smiled, and he suspected that she already knew the answer.

"It was your scent, of course," he smiled back. "Not just your normal smell, but…that, together with the *special addition*. Something that told me – screamed at me – that now was a good time."

She sat up and turned towards him, and then in a smooth operation, parted her legs and sat across his lap. She grinned down at him from her elevated position. "You could smell that?" she said, squirming a little.

"Anyone with half a nose could've probably smelled it," he replied, trying to remain serious. "It's just that I can…"

Mary squirmed some more. "Can you smell anything now?" she asked.

"I can," he replied. "Very much so." He closed his eyes. "But it's more a matter of touch at the moment," he said, looking like a Cheshire cat, and reaching up to her.

Chapter 4

Derek reached for a magazine on the waiting-room table. He looked at the front cover, put it back on the table, stood up, walked over to a cheap print hanging on the wall, examined it, and then came back and sat down next to Mary again. He stayed there for about five seconds and then once more made a move to get up. Mary grabbed his arm and pulled him down. She didn't say anything, not even softly, but the look on her face was enough. He tried to sit still, and to concentrate.

It was now three weeks since the accident, and his enhanced sense of smell was still with him – hadn't diminished one iota. A few things associated with it had changed, however. To start with, the number of smells he could now identify had increased enormously. From the very beginning, he'd been amazed by the variety of scents and aromas that he seemed to just 'know' from past experience. But there'd also been a great many that he couldn't recognize, that he could only make sense of if he saw where they were coming from. And this had been happening constantly since he got out of hospital. Also, he was now able to better differentiate between what could only be called 'shades' of a scent: the slight variations of a basic or 'signature' odour that contained so much information about the state of the emitter. In the case of people and some animals, he could now not only tell if they were asleep or awake, happy or sad, friendly or angry, but also – crudely – something about the extents of these qualities.

And then there were the behavioural changes that Derek was aware of – sometimes. Changes in himself, that is. He still had to grapple with the urges that some scents seemed to trigger; urges that might take control of his actions. Just a few days ago he had frightened the life out of Mary when he suddenly swerved off the road as they were driving home. He had detected the aroma of pancakes and maple syrup – the real stuff – coming from a motor home in Ditchley's Caravan Park. His mental guard was down, like it often is when you're driving a familiar route, and zapo! He just went for it. Missing lunch that day probably hadn't helped either. It was all over in less than half a minute – Mary's yelling and cursing had brought him to his senses pretty quickly – but it was a good example of the sort of thing that happened when he wasn't thinking; when the conscious part of his mind wasn't in control.

The other aspect of his behaviour – the one that Mary was now alluding to with her eyes here in the specialist's waiting room – was similar to the first, but a bit subtler. And unlike the major cases of being overwhelmed, of which there hadn't been many, Derek usually wasn't aware of what he was doing – not until it was pointed out to him. These were the small but urgent actions that often seemed to occupy him now – not all the time mind, but enough to be noticeable to others. It mainly happened when he didn't have a particular job or task to perform – like now. One of the plethora of aromas wafting around him would grab his attention, and if it seemed to require further investigation, then that's what he'd do. It might be a different sort of rubber in a car tyre, so he'd go and check it out – go for a closer sniff. And while he was doing that he might detect an unusual odour coming from a drain near the car, so he'd walk over and do a bit of nose-work around that area. Then a woman might walk by who was wearing a dress that had some exotic threads in it, so he'd follow her for a few steps trying to inhale more of the fragrance. In other words, he couldn't sit still once this state of smell curiosity took hold – it'd be one after another, bang, bang, bang. It didn't take much to break the pattern: someone calling out to him, or something non-osmatic – visual for example – grabbing his attention. Like Mary had just done now.

"Was I doing it again?" he asked softly, dropping back onto the metal-framed chair, and looking at the four other people sitting around the room.

Mary nodded. She didn't speak but her smile showed understanding.

"The wood in that picture frame is cypress pine," he whispered. "Could smell it from down the corridor. And the kids' play table over there in the corner has got something I can't identify on it – I think it's those funny looking coloured pens. And that old man's coat…"

Mary squeezed his arm. "It's all right Derek," she said in a low voice. "The world will keep turning." He frowned at her. "I mean you don't have to go running around investigating everything that catches your fancy," she added. He frowned even more.

At that moment, a woman who looked like she might be a nurse, entered the room from one of its three doors. "Mister Sadler?" she said, looking at Derek.

"Yeah, that's right," Derek said as he stood. "How'd ya know it was me?"

The woman didn't answer but held out her hand. "Hello, I'm Susan Haldane, the olfactory specialist…the smell doctor."

Derek shook her hand while getting to his feet; he noticed her youth and her freckly face. "Oh, yeah, Richard whatsisname said there'd be an expert from Brisbane here to have a look at me today."

She grinned. "Yes, well, Doctor Barrington is on the phone at the moment but he asked that I come and get you." She then introduced herself to Mary, and led the couple into one of the consulting rooms. Mary scowled at her husband and mouthed the word 'Barrington'. He knew that they'd been talking about him earlier in the day – and over the last couple of weeks – but he'd just forgotten the guy's surname. He thought it was probably the unexpected introduction by this pretty young doctor that had got him a bit flustered. He hoped that was the reason. But he'd been forgetting a few things lately, and…

"Ahh! Mister and Missus Sadler, how are you both today?" Barrington, the surgeon who'd treated Derek after his accident put the phone down as he spoke, his greeting interrupting Derek's train of thought. "Now, I assume you've met Doctor Haldane," he said. "She's come all the way from Brisbane with her gadget," he pointed to a device of some kind near the window, "just to examine you – to see if we can sort out what's going on." He smiled.

Derek was extremely grateful to 'Doctor Green-eyes' – Mary had called him that once – because of his expertise and professionalism in treating him after the accident. But, for all his cleverness, he was still sceptical about the veracity of Derek's incredibly heightened smelling ability, and particularly the interpretive part – the part where Derek could identify not only signature smells of people and things, but also something about their current state.

He was willing to accept that the boatbuilder's sense of smell had, perhaps, become a little more acute – in a fairly basic and straightforward sort of way. But he wasn't having any part of what Derek had told him about the *degree* of sensitivity, or about the level of meaning that he was now capable of putting on many of the scents that he could perceive. He'd even suggested that the next step might be an appointment with a psychiatrist. It was at this point that Derek had told him he could go fuck himself. He'd not given this advice in a particularly angry voice, just how he would've told anyone in the boatyard who might question his honesty or intelligence. Wisely, Barrington had backed away from that idea and had decided to follow a more scientific approach – to first see whether his patient did, in fact, have *hyperosmia*, an abnormally acute sense of smell. Derek appreciated the trouble the man was going to – Barrington didn't even have to keep him as a patient at this stage – but still, he didn't like the scepticism, the disbelief. The truth was, he'd stopped giving all the details of his condition to the surgeon, no longer feeling that he could fully trust him. In fact, at this stage, it wouldn't take much for Derek to actually start disliking Doctor Green-eyes.

"So, this is the olfactometer," Susan-the-smell-doctor was saying. Derek was still mulling over the conversation they'd been having for the last fifteen minutes. He liked this woman. Besides smelling fresh and happy, she seemed to have an aura of sympathy and honesty – nothing to do with her scent, although he could never be sure of such a thing anymore, smells now being so influential in his overall perceptions. But more than these attributes, he liked her because she showed a willingness to accept that perhaps his abilities were all real rather than simply a mix of real and imagined or, as Barrington still appeared to think, totally imaginary. "Mister Sadler…"

"Oh, yeah, sorry, off with the fairies," he said.

"This is the olfactometer," she repeated. "I won't go into detail about how it works, but it's computer controlled and is normally used to establish the strength of particular odours."

Derek stared at the stainless steel rig. It looked like two boxes on top of one another, each about the size of a portable tool chest, and each with a sloping upper face. The boxes were held in a frame that had two wheels at the bottom – like a warehouse trolley. There was an LCD screen on the sloping surface of the top box, and two tubes coming out of the bottom box – each being connected to what looked like big, plastic ice cream cones. There was also a cylinder of compressed air next to the instrument.

"You're gunna get me to stick my nose into one of those cones, aren't ya?" he said.

"Well, into each of them, actually," she replied. "But let me explain how our little activity here today will be a bit different to how we normally use this machine." She smiled as Derek nodded and looked across at his wife.

"As I said before, the olfactometer is most commonly used to determine the relative strengths of odours – usually bad ones."

"Geez, Susan, you and that machine could settle a few arguments between some o'me mates down on the coast." Derek grinned but noticed that Mary was giving him her 'you're-being-uncouth' look. Barrington, who was still at his desk, chuckled.

"Believe me, Derek, I've heard similar suggestions many times before." The young specialist had a sparkle in her eye that told him that she may indeed have used the machine for certain 'unofficial' measurements of the anal kind – probably amongst her medico mates during a lab piss-up. That sparkle made him like her even more. He also appreciated how she silently agreed to move from formal names to first names. "Anyway," she continued, "we normally use a jury with the olfactometer. They're just a group of ordinary people – nothing special about their senses of smell – who go through a process of sniffing different dilutions of an odour. Each time, they compare what they consider its strength to be, to that of a standard neutral odour whose strength we can control precisely. We have to use a jury because smell is such a subjective thing." She saw that Derek didn't fully understand – his lips slightly puckered and his eyebrows angled. "What I mean…" she looked at Mary, obviously wanting to include her in the explanation, "…is that people perceive smells differently – particularly when it comes to how strong a certain smell is – or how attractive or how repulsive a smell might be. In such cases, we have to rely on a sort of average perception from a group of people."

"The jury," Derek said.

"That's right," she affirmed. "But today we'll be using a different process. Rather than having a jury and trying to establish the strength of a particular smell, I'll be linking up the machine to a set of smells that we've already got a lot of information about. For each one, we can deliver a range of strengths, from well below what is considered the threshold of detection by humans, right up to quite intense levels. I'll also see how you rate the strengths compared to the standard that we use."

"What, you mean like a three-day-old dead sardine in a forty-four gallon drum?" Derek asked.

She smiled and cocked her head a little to one side. Derek got the distinct impression she was conveying the message 'you're a lot sharper than I thought'. "An interesting idea, but too hard to control I would think. We use the chemical, butanol, as a reference odour – over a wide range of strengths. That's part of what the olfactometer does via its computer."

"So the sardine idea isn't a goer?" Derek said, enjoying himself.

"No," she replied. "Right concept but needs refinement. I think we'll stick with butanol if that's okay."

Derek wanted to say something about his suggested standard probably attracting too many cats anyway, but decided not to push his luck. "So what do I do?" he said.

The young redhead flicked on a switch and pressed her finger on various parts of the machine's screen. "Touch sensitive," she said when she glanced towards him and saw his interest. Again, Derek thought about responding with a smart answer, but he could see Mary out of the corner of his eye, and thought better of it. At first he was surprised by his urge to flirt – it wasn't something he usually did. But then he realized it was something to do with the woman's scent; it contained a touch of encouragement. He gave his head a little shake, to reset his thoughts.

"Are you all right?" she asked.

"Yeah, fine," he said, "just anxious to get started."

"Okay, now I want you to begin by breathing ultra pure air." She handed him a mask that was connected to the bottom of the olfactometer. "Just breathe normally, and when the machine beeps, place your nose into here and inhale," she held up one of the plastic ice cream cones. "And then simply tell me whether you can definitely detect a smell, or think you might be able to detect one but aren't sure, or definitely can't detect anything. After that, I want you to place your nose in this other cone, and do the same thing, but this time, if you can detect an odour, tell me whether it's stronger, about the same, or weaker than that in the first cone – even though the smells might be totally different in make-up."

"'cause one's the reference, right?"

"Yes, that's correct," she said, holding up the first cone. "This one. We'll start with the lowest concentration possible, and work our way up until you detect something." She then pointed to the second cone. "And with this one, when you do smell something, I want you to describe or identify it as best you can." Derek nodded; it sounded simple enough. "Also," she went on, "with each new smell cycle I'll get you to breathe the ultra pure air again – it'll bring your nasal mucous membranes back to a zero excitation level."

"Flush out my sniffer, huh?" he said as he took the mask from her. This first part alone was going to be interesting; even after just three weeks, he couldn't imagine breathing without smelling something. He placed the mask over his nose. Immediately, he detected the plastic of the connecting tubes, and also the steel of the air cylinder, but both were quite weak. He looked across at Mary and jiggled his eyebrows. It brought a smile to her lips. She looked so pretty when she smiled. What a woman. She didn't have to be here, but had insisted on accompanying him – 'I want to understand as much as I can about what's going on with you,' she had said while gently squeezing his arm. He looked over to where Barrington had been sitting, but he was gone – nowhere in the room. Then the machine made its little beeping sound.

He removed the mask from his face and replaced it with the cone that Susan handed him. He inhaled the air and immediately detected an alcohol-like smell – faint but obvious. "Definitely," he said to the specialist, and then took the other cone from her. The smell from this one was also weak but, again, noticeable – more noticeable in fact. "Bananas," he said, "and quite a bit stronger than the reference." He removed the cone from his face. Susan was frowning, and looking at the screen.

"It can't be the machine," she said, almost to herself. "I checked it out just before you arrived."

"So did I do something wrong?" he said.

"No, no…it's just that…" she pressed various parts of the screen. "It's just that you've detected the reference at 0.001 parts per million, no one ever detects that." She looked up at him, worried. "And the banana odour…it's way below the detection threshold." She looked back at the screen. "Let's continue on; recalibration would take too long, and there seems little point…" She suddenly stopped and looked around. "Mary, would you come over here? I'd like to see what result we get with *you* if we repeat this first measurement."

It took almost an hour and a half to do the testing, and Derek had been relieved when Susan said they were finished. He and Mary had gone to the hospital cafeteria to have an early lunch while Susan did a preliminary analysis of the results. She was returning to Brisbane that evening, and wanted to 'sort a few things out' regarding the figures as soon as possible. This, apparently, was to include making some phone calls to a couple of other specialists, as well as discussing some of her findings with Barrington. Both Derek and his wife were fairly sure that the lady with the olfactometer had probably confirmed scientifically what they both knew from everyday experience. Derek was fully aware, just within himself, of what he was capable of. And Mary, well, she couldn't get inside her husband's nose, or his head, but she had seen enough confirming evidence of what he'd said he could smell. She'd long ago given up the idea that it was all just some weird fantasy.

"It obviously dawned on her that you were for real when you did the very first test," Mary said as she raised her pie-laden fork to her mouth.

"No, I think she thought her smellometer was on the blink at first," Derek replied. "It was only after you had a go that she went all quiet and professional. How many steps did you have to go through before you could smell anything? – was it four?"

"Five," she replied. " And she did mutter something about my response being normal."

Derek looked down at his plate, an expression of disgust on his face. "Jesus, these fucking chips aren't normal," he said – they're not even warm; and they taste like they've been re-heated every day since the dinosaurs were here." He held his knife and fork vertically on the table, trying to decide whether to continue eating.

"I don't think they had chips back then," Mary replied while cutting into her meat pie. "What's your pasty like? – my pie's fine."

Derek picked up his plate, and looked across at the servery area. "Bloody hospital cafeterias; I'm gunna take this back." He stood up. Then he saw Doctors Haldane and Barrington enter the large, almost unoccupied eating room, so he sat down again. They hurried towards him and Mary.

"Derek, Mary, I know this is a bit unusual, but I wonder if Doctor Barrington and I could have a chat with you here about your results." She was looking at Derek. "I've just found out that I'll have to leave for Brisbane earlier than planned – if I want to get a flight at all. So I haven't got a lot of time, but I really do want to talk to you about what this morning's testing revealed."

"And perhaps I might need to rethink my ideas about what's happening with you," added Barrington.

Derek spread his arms and hands, indicating the two chairs at either end of the table.

As the surgeon sat, he glanced down at Derek's plate. "Oh, I see you ordered the chips; aren't they foul?"

"Like a chook pen," Derek replied.

Susan rolled out a long sheet of computer printout paper in front of her – it had graphs and text and numbers on it as well as sporadic notes in blue handwriting. "Let me put it in a nutshell, Derek," she said looking up from the paper. You correctly identified all but one of the twenty-five odours – and that one was problematic. Now, that degree of accuracy is unusual but certainly not unheard of. What *is* almost unheard of, though, is your threshold for detecting and correctly identifying the test odours. I've certainly never seen anything like it, nor have two of my senior colleagues who I phoned. There's only been a couple of cases of such extreme hyperosmia in the literature as far as any of us are aware, and they were on the other side of the planet and not in recent times." She stared at Derek. "You've still got the same forty million receptor cells for smelling, just like the rest of us, but something extraordinary seems to have happened either with how your brain deals with the receptor output, or with the chemistry and physics of the receptors themselves… Or maybe both, or… There are all sorts of possibilities I suppose; there are so many steps in the processing sequence – and we don't understand some of them at all."

Barrington leaned forward. "What the data suggests, Mister Sadler, is that your accident, rather than inducing *anosmia* – no sense of smell, which isn't uncommon in some types of head injuries – has led to an amazing hyperosmia. I mean, you seem to have a sensitivity akin to that of some other species, but we have no idea why. My German shepherd has fifty times more olfactory receptors than you, but you probably have the same degree of sensitivity as him!" The other three noticed the increase in pitch in the surgeon's voice.

"Well, we don't know that – we don't have any comparative data," Susan said frowning at her colleague. "But it has just occurred to me that we need to check out the other assumption you've just verbalised – I made it too…"

"What?" Barrington said, "that he's got the same number of receptors as the rest of us?" He chuckled. "You're not suggesting that Mister Sadler has suddenly grown more receptors, are you?"

"Maybe he had them all the time but they weren't being used," Susan responded, clearly annoyed at the derisive tone in Barrington's voice. "Or maybe the stem cells in his epithelium have started converting at a much faster rate than the usual forty days."

"Yes, but where would all the extra merchandise go?" Barrington shot back, not so patronising now. "Are you talking about more cilia per neuron, or more neurons? And what about the mitral cells in the olfactory bulb? Are they going to…"

At this point Derek lifted one of his hands in the air. "Excuse me my learned friends, but you lost me a few sentences back." The others stopped speaking and turned towards him. "And it is me that you're talking about."

"Yes, he's sitting right here in front of you," Mary added, glad of the opportunity to chastise members of a profession who she thought were, by and large, far too high and mighty for their own good.

"I am sorry, Derek," Susan said. She glanced at Barrington; there was an unmistakable flash of anger in her eyes. "Doctor Barrington and I really don't need to discuss in front of you our differing ideas about what might be causing these results."

Derek looked at the surgeon. "But at least you're now willing to admit that I'm not making all this up?"

"I never thought that, Mister Sadler," Barrington replied. "What I did think was that the most likely explanation of your symptoms was *parosmia* – that you were perceiving odours that weren't actually present."

"And now?" Mary said.

Barrington looked across at her. "Well, like I said before, these olfactometer results have forced me to reconsider that diagnosis; your husband clearly has a real, and at least partly measurable, capability – and it is truly extraordinary." He then turned to his colleague. "But we obviously have a lot of thinking to do if we're to even come close to explaining what's happening with him."

"And more investigating," Susan added, looking at Derek. "We would really like to do some exploratory work with you."

"I don't think I like the sound of that," Derek said. "What sort of exploring do you wanna do?"

"Well, to start with, I think we should arrange for you to be checked out with a nasal endoscope," the redhead said. Derek felt a shiver pass through him. Five years earlier, he'd had a colonoscopy – a probe stuck up his arse so a doctor could examine his large intestine. They found nothing, but his colon had gone into spasm at the beginning of the procedure while he was still conscious. He just about went berserk with pain there on the operating table before they managed to get enough extra anaesthetic into him. All in all, it was an event that his body and mind would never forget.

"Susan," he said in the politest of voices, "I'm sure there are lots of places you could stick your endoscope, but my nose is not going to be one of them."

She was obviously surprised by his remark, and a little flustered by the relaxed expression on his face. "But…" she ventured. Mary interrupted.

"I wouldn't push it my dear," she said coldly, knowing the probable nature of her husband's response.

Susan looked at Barrington who simply spread his palms in a gesture of 'don't-ask-me'. But she recovered quickly. "All right," she said, "what about an MRI or CAT scan – nothing intrusive?" She saw Derek's hesitancy. "I really would like to study you more," she added. "We might find out a great deal about both the sense of smell and the functioning of the brain." There was a beseeching look in her eyes – as if she recognized how close he was to getting up and leaving. "And I would also like to talk to you about the effect your disorder is having on your day-to-day existence, and your life in general."

Derek had liked her scent from the beginning, even though she tried to mask it with an expensive and, for him, overly powerful perfume. And now there was a touch of something else added to her suppressed signature odour; it matched the pleading undertone that accompanied her words. He found it attractive. And the idea of discussing the deeper, more personal aspects of how his life had shifted sideways as a result of his new ability…it had a certain appeal; especially since she was an olfactory specialist – and from outside his circle of family and friends. It might be beneficial to talk personally with someone like this, a dispassionate expert. But he didn't see how he could afford the time. "Well, we'll see," he said. "I'd like to help, but there are a few problems."

"What problems?" Susan said.

"Well, to start with, you're normally down in Brisbane, and I'm up here, eight hundred kilometres away. Besides that, I have a business to run. Every minute I'm away being tested or examined or even just coming here to the hospital, is money lost for me. Either that or I have to try finding the time from somewhere else to finish my work. And it's usually the family who suffer when I start doin' that sort of thing – I've been doin' too much of it already. Anyway, I'm not sure that I wanna be studied in the first place."

Susan blinked, you could see she was trying to formulate a response that would take into account what Derek had just said, without shutting the door on the possibility of further investigation. But it was Barrington who spoke next.

"Of course, these are all valid points, Mister Sadler," he said. "What I suggest is that you go home and think about the contribution to science and medicine you might be able to make by being involved in an investigative program…and Doctor Haldane and I will think of how we might address your concerns. And then we'll get back to you."

To Derek, the doctor's words might've sounded entirely reasonable, except for the patronizing tone that accompanied them. He glanced over to his wife. She had her lips tight together, in a way that he recognized. She was pissed off too. He pushed his chair back from the table and sniffed. Susan looked at him. That attractive addition to her scent was no longer present. "We'll see," he said.

They were only twenty kilometres from home when Derek finally wound up the window. Lately, he enjoyed being in the passenger seat with the window down. The constant rush and renewal of scents was exhilarating, and captivating too – like when you're flying in a small plane and looking down upon the ever-changing landscape below. But in Derek's case, it was the multitude of scents and aromas that vied for his attention rather than anything perceived by his eyes: the lemon-scented gums that lined the road, hay bales in the fields beyond, cicadas searching for a mate, decaying bodies of wallaby roadkill; birds, rocks, flowers, people, cars – all with delicate variations in tint and tone. After a while, though, it became too much for him, and he had to have a break or the pleasure would turn into a mild sort of nausea – nothing drastic, but unpleasant all the same.

The muffled blurting of the VW's engine took on a more subdued timbre as the window seated itself at the top of the door frame – still loud but now allowing the occupants to speak and to be heard.

"Had enough?" Mary said as she slowed down to take a tight curve.

"No, your driving has improved a lot in recent weeks," he replied, pretending to be preoccupied with his thoughts.

"I mean have you had enough of the odoriferous kaleidoscope?" She glanced across at him and saw him grinning. "Smart arse," she added.

"You use a word like 'odoriferous kaleidoscope' and you call *me* a smart arse?" he said, still grinning.

"It's two words, and what do you expect? I'm an

English teacher," she replied, eyes on the road, smile on her mouth.

Derek didn't respond with words but reached out his hand and began to gently twirl the hair at the nape of his wife's neck. When they were younger, she had always liked him doing that if she was driving and he was next to her, but they hadn't followed the practice for some years – until this moment. Mary didn't look at him or say anything, but she did tilt her head back slightly and slowly turned it a little from side to side. While doing this, she closed and opened her eyes in a series of extended blinks.

"Just don't get us killed," Derek said as he kept up the twirling, happy at her reaction.

"If we crash it'll be your fault, not mine," she replied dreamily.

"Should I stop?" he asked, pausing the movement of his hand.

"Don't you dare," she replied, nuzzling his fingers with the back of her head.

They drove on for several minutes in silence. Derek wanted to think about some of the issues that had arisen at the hospital only a short time ago. But it was difficult to concentrate. Some other part of his mind was urging him to just sit back and fondle his mate while taking in the odour-filled vista that was presenting itself to him. Thinking – the higher order kind at least – didn't seem so important at times like these. He knew that he'd been giving in to his more basic compulsions of late. It had bothered him in the beginning, but not so much now. As long as he could remain in control and not do anything too embarrassing, that was the main thing. But even then, he wasn't as concerned as before. Bugger it, it all required just too much conscious thought processing. Anyway, there was now an interesting and familiar scent filling the interior of the car. A favourite.

"What did you think of that woman doctor's use of the word 'disorder' when she was talking about your smelling ability?" Mary said, breaking the silence and interrupting the sensual flow that Derek was becoming lost in.

"Huh?"

"You know, she said your heightened sensitivity and identification abilities were a *disorder*."

Derek blinked. Several seconds ticked by while he focused his thoughts. "I dunno, it probably doesn't matter what she calls it…I don't really care."

"Okay, but what about it's implications?" She shrugged her shoulders, indicating that he should stop playing with her hair and concentrate on what she was saying.

He moved his hand back from her head but kept it in place at the top of the seat. "What implications?" he said, his rational side now becoming dominant.

"Well, what you can now do with your sense of smell *is* the result of an accident, so in that regard it *is* a disorder." He nodded. "But the things you can do are amazing – you have a capability far beyond what most other people seem to have; maybe beyond anybody…ever."

"So…?"

"So how can that be a disorder? I mean in the usual sense of the word?" Derek didn't respond, he knew when she was on a roll. "But it's not even the use of the word – you could probably justify that; dis-order: out of the ordinary. It's the notion of being unwell in one sense, and…I don't know…extra well in another sense. It's a paradox." She pulled on the steering wheel to take another curve. After straightening out again, she looked across at him. "You're a living paradox," she said.

"I'm sure it happens all the time," Derek replied, bowing his head to look up through the windscreen at the clouds – his nose having suggested they might drop some rain.

"Well I've never heard of anything like this happening before," Mary said in protest.

"Sure you have," Derek responded. "Just think of Darcy Jacobson over at Maccleville. Remember what an arsehole he was when he was a builder? Ripping off anyone he could con into hiring him, and doing shoddy work when he was forced into doing anything at all. Always fuckin' arguing and fighting. Nobody liked him – not even his own family."

Mary nodded. "Until his accident," she said.

"That's right, until his accident. The day he found he

would never walk again, something else happened too. At first, people thought they were dealin' with a new person who just looked like Darcy but was in a wheelchair. The change was incredible. And now, you couldn't meet a nicer bloke: always courteous, listens to what you have to say, and will help you if he thinks you need help… Look what he did for those kids at the special school in town, used a big swag of his insurance money for that centre."

"And his wife…what's her name…Deidre – she started being a lot happier too," Mary added. "I remember how dreadful she used to look when you'd see her in town – you know, troubled; bags under her eyes, silent, frowning. But now, God! She looks great. Always bright and cheerful, chatting away to people in the street – she says 'hello' to me even though we don't really know each other. And he's usually with her too, rolling along in his wheelchair. You never used to see them together in the past."

Derek inhaled, paused for a moment, and then started fingering Mary's hair again. "Yeah, well, anyway, the point I was trying to make is…is…oh fuck…what were we talking about?"

"The point you're making is that there are cases of other people who have developed a special – and positive – capability because of an injury. Their unwellness in one sense has made them well in another."

"That's right, and I'm sure there are lots of other people who have had their lives somehow improved because of accidents – and the lives of those around them too. Darcy can't be the only one." Derek's nostrils were filled with that scent again. It was hard to stay focused on the conversation, even though he was interested.

"That's a pretty deep thought, Darling," Mary said as she again relished the feel of his fingers in her hair and on her neck. 'Darling' was an old pet name she had only started using again recently.

"Well, I'm just a deep sort of guy, aren't I?" he replied as he found himself giving way to the scent – smooth and sumptuous and oceanic.

"But you're different to lots of other people because you haven't lost any capability – you've still got all your arms and legs, and you can think clearly…and do nice things with your fingers…" She giggled, and for a moment realized how much she appreciated another aspect of her husband's behaviour that seemed to be related to his accident – to his smell sensitivity.

"Why don't you take a left at that dirt track up ahead," he said softly and close to her ear. "I'm sure there'll be a secluded place off there somewhere." She smiled and changed gears. Derek knew he could have made the point that maybe there wasn't an overall gain in what had happened to him; that maybe he was losing something; as though there was a price to pay for his extraordinary capability. But he didn't want to think about it anymore; that special smell of his wife was just too inviting.

Chapter 5

Doolies Beach is only a few kilometres south of the Yuragan township – just off the road that leads to Ross Harbour and the yacht club. There are lots of beaches in the area, but this one, a broad strip of sand about a kilometre long between two rocky outcrops, was Derek's favourite. Probably Rifkin's too. What had once been just an occasional romp had now become a regular early morning activity. It meant that Derek would start work a little later than he used to but that didn't really bother him – not like it would've done before the accident.

And this really was a beautiful beach. It faced the remnants of the big ocean swells that broke on the Great Barrier Reef – well beyond the horizon; and several small, nearby islands also provided some protection. Sometimes the waves were big enough to bodysurf, but at other times, when there hadn't been much wind, there'd be just a tiny shore break. These were the times when Rifkin would rejoice in retrieving sticks or balls or old thongs that Derek would throw into the water. He'd bark excitedly when his owner walked towards the water carrying a throwing object, and then stand there, up to his belly, looking out to sea – waiting for the object to go flying over his head and into view. Then he'd be off, paddling away with all fours, and somehow giving the front half of his body a boost up when a foaming wave hit; it'd slow him down for a second or two but then he'd be off again, paddling like his life depended on it. On the days when the onshore breeze was up – usually from the southeast, except in the really hot months when it came from the northeast – Rifkin would still get excited by the *idea* of retrieving something from the water, but then he'd look around at Derek with an expression that said 'those waves are pretty fucking big, boss; you don't *really* expect me to go out through all that shit do you?' Occasionally, Derek would try to cajole his companion into braving this bigger stuff, but usually he understood the dog's point of view and wouldn't insist; wouldn't even go down to the water's edge.

In fact, he'd come to understand Rifkin's point of view about a number of things lately – that's how he felt anyway. Like today, for instance. Here was the dog, nose in the air, obviously onto something interesting. Derek could smell it too – a bird, several birds, but not the seagulls that usually stood on the rocks or at the high-water mark. The scent was coming from behind the grass-covered primary dune that rose from the back of the beach – from somewhere amongst the sheoaks that lined the elevated foreshore. Rifkin turned to Derek, seeming to know that his human companion was equally aware of the odour. It was as though the dog was waiting for permission to investigate – like Derek was the alpha male of a two-member pack. The thing is, though, Derek understood – as with many things of late – not with his rational mind but with some other, more primitive part of his brain. He too found the scent intriguing and worthy of investigation. He gave a slight nod, and Rifkin was off; so was he; dog first, human second – both heading for the dune and the trees beyond.

As they ran up the sand, and then along one of the sand-and-soil tracks, a loud squawking filled the breeze. Almost immediately, there was a flurry of movement from the low branches of a nearby sheoak, and four black cockatoos rose into the air, still calling loudly. Rifkin lifted his front paws onto the tree's trunk and looked up at the circling birds. At the same time, Derek grabbed at a dark, shiny feather that drifted down from above. The dog saw this and gave up his skyward gaze to see what it was that his chase companion had managed to grab. He jumped up on Derek, just as he had on the tree trunk, and sniffed the feather that was offered him. After examining its odour, he attempted to take it in his mouth but Derek pulled it away and placed it under his own nose. The smell was strong: oily and earthy, with a characteristic bird-meat undertone, but also quite unique in its overall signature. He examined it with his eyes and then lifted it to his nose again; slowly pulling it horizontally under his nostrils, and sniffing loudly. When he did this, his mind filled with images of black cockatoos – just like the real ones that continued to circle overhead. But the images in his head weren't only visual; they were also to do with smell and sound and even the feel of the feather and the taste of bird flesh – even though he'd only ever eaten chicken and turkey. He sighed and then handed the feather to Rifkin again. The dog gladly took it in his mouth and immediately turned around and walked back to the beach.

As they both descended the track through the dune, Derek noticed an old lady wearing a floppy, green bush hat walking towards them. He'd seen her before on the beach and had always greeted her with a 'good morning' but she'd never replied, except with a scowl.

"Oh no," she said, pointing at Rifkin as she stepped closer. "You let him kill one of the cockies. How could you?!"

"No, dear, it's just a feather he picked up from the ground." It was a little lie but Derek thought it would minimize any further discussion.

"Then why are they still making their distress calls?" She pointed towards a more distant tree where the cockatoos had settled, and where they continued to squawk.

Derek followed her finger. At the same time, he

noticed that Rifkin was now lying on the sand, back legs splayed out and the feather sticking up between his front paws. "Ah, they're always carrying on like that; it doesn't mean one of them's been hurt; they're just noisy buggers."

The old lady raised herself to full height, stiffening her shoulders and pouting her lips. "Actually, they're Red-tailed Black-Cockatoos, *Calyptorhynchus banksii*, she said, "and I am quite familiar with their cries, and what we're hearing is their distress call."

Old or not, Derek was becoming a little annoyed. "Well if that screeching is their distress call then I'm not surprised, look!" He pointed down at Rifkin who was chewing his feather, "there's a potential predator nearby." Then he wished he hadn't used the word 'predator', and quickly added, "But he didn't get anywhere near one of the birds."

The old lady pulled down on her hat. "Is that so? Well I saw you running up the sand dune with your dog, and it looked very much like you were encouraging him to attack."

Derek suddenly felt uncomfortable, she was too close to the truth. "Oh that's just plain silly," he said. "And besides, Rifkin wouldn't know how to attack anything, not even...not even if he'd been to attack training school." The woman stared at him. *What a stupid thing to say*, he thought to himself. "Anyway, I have to go," he said. "Enjoy your walk." After taking several dozen steps, he glanced back and saw that the woman had climbed to the top of the dune and was heading for where he and Rifkin had been. "Look at that," he said to the dog, "old biddy, doesn't fucking believe me."

Ten minutes later, after a short session of 'I throw, you retrieve', Derek was approaching the rocks at the southern end of the beach when it occurred to him that Rifkin, who was up ahead, had been spending an unusual amount of time examining a particular spot on the sand. As he got closer, he saw that it was a series of rough smudges and lines and paw prints that was holding his dog's attention. He then caught the smell himself; a number of smells. They were dog scents; three, maybe four; each with it's own signature but also with high amounts of other, subsidiary odours. These conjured up feelings of fear, aggression, desperation. Some sort of fight had occurred here – probably earlier in the morning. Derek was intrigued, but it was all a bit confused. He walked in a small circle around the area, making short inhalations and tilting his head, trying to match the visual images of the sand to those originating from somewhere in his nose. There was more to know though. Suddenly he dropped to his knees so he could be closer to the odours. That made it clearer...and the spot on the ground where Rifkin currently had his snout, some fascinating scents were coming from there: of canine flesh and urine and...what was it...saliva? The sensory images of what had happened were beginning to form in his mind but were still indistinct. He crawled over on all fours to join his dog, nose close to the sand, totally focused, enthralled.

"What on earth are you doing?"

Derek's attention suddenly leaped back from what seemed like another universe. He looked up and saw the old woman. She was leaning forward, hands on her hips, searching the sand with her eyes. "Is there something buried there?" she said.

He scrambled to his feet, wiping at the sand that was sprinkled across the end of his nose. "Oh…oh, I just wanted to get a better look at a bug that was down there," he said.

"Where?" She frowned as she temporarily transferred her gaze from the sand to him.

"Oh…it must've flown away," he said. Before she could respond, he looked at his wristwatch and added, "My God! It's later than I thought; I really have to go. Bye." He walked briskly across the rocks towards the track that would take him to the roadside parking area where he'd left the van – Rifkin was beside him. Glancing back, he saw the woman still in the same place, and still leaning over looking at the sand. He rarely lied – hated it in fact, but today he'd done it several times to that old woman. They weren't big ones, of course. And he only told them because the truth would've seemed too strange – probably would've frightened the old thing. Besides, how could you explain in a few seconds of early morning chitchat something so unusual and complicated – particularly to someone you don't even know? Still, he felt sick with himself; lying was not a good thing to do at any time, fuckit – even if it was to protect the sensibilities of an old lady or, and this annoyed him a lot more, even if it was to avoid his own embarrassment. Bugger it, he wouldn't do that again. Tell the truth and stuff the consequences – he had nothing to be ashamed of.

The drive back to the house was always an enjoyable time for both of them. Derek sniffing the onrushing air on one side of the van, and Rifkin with his head out the window on the other. Sometimes one of them would get a whiff of a strange scent and, after examining it for a moment, would turn to the other to see if he had also detected it. At least that's what Derek thought Rifkin was doing when the dog would turn his head back into the van with a curious expression on his face, and then promptly turn his snout back into the wind. Derek always smiled on these occasions, heartened that there was someone with whom he could share his new experiences – who sort of understood – even if it was just a mongrel dog.

They'd turned off the main Yuragan-to-Trelborough road a few minutes ago and were heading down the narrow strip of bitumen called Mendelson's Lane, towards home, when Derek noticed a white car parked next to his dirt driveway – almost in the drainage ditch. As he turned into the driveway he noticed 'Northern Tribune' written on the side of the car. He put the van in neutral and pulled on the sloppy handbrake. "Can I help you mate?" he called from the window to the approaching figure – a man of about fifty dressed in a white shirt and tie, and grey trousers. He also had a camera hanging from a strap around his neck.

"You can if you're Mister Sadler – Derek Sadler, that is." The man smiled.

Derek scanned him with his eyes. The shirt had seen better days, and the tie appeared to have been hastily put on – the knot looked like shit and it was way off centre. And there was something in the man's odour that he didn't like – couldn't quite put his finger on it but it made him wary. "See the name on the side of the van?" he said, and he waited for the man to glance down, "Well that's me."

"Ah, yes, well Mister Sadler, I'm Rohan Sinclair from the *Northern Tribune*, and I wondered whether I could have a word with you? I believe you have quite a story to tell." He smiled, and his smell got worse – and suddenly Rifkin barked.

"Jesus Rifkin!" Derek said as he turned around. The dog had his front paws on the gearbox well and was glaring across his master's body at the stranger – a low, rumbling growl coming from his throat. Derek held up a finger and Rifkin sat down, but the dog's eyes stayed fixed on the stranger, and the growl continued. Derek turned back to the *Tribune* man who had now moved a little further away from the van. "Are you a reporter?" Derek asked, having to speak more loudly.

"Yes, that's right," he said, still smiling but with that slight look of concern about being ripped to pieces that you sometimes notice in people's eyes when you're accompanied by a moderately large, growling meat eater. "I was wondering if we could have a chat for a few minutes – maybe in my car – away from your dog."

Derek pulled his head in from the window and leaned across Rifkin. He wound up the passenger-side window – leaving a gap at the top – and then did the same on his side. He then got out of the van, cautioning Rifkin to stay where he was. After slamming the door, he turned to the reporter. "We can talk here," he said. "Now what's this all about?"

"Mister Sadler – can I call you Derek?...

"Tell you what," Derek said, "why don't you answer my question before worrying about what to fuckin' call me." He'd encountered *Tribune* reporters a couple of times before in his life and had never enjoyed the outcome. He especially remembered how his words had been twisted by one sleazy arsehole who had attended his father's funeral – ostensibly to pay his respects to a well-known local figure. The piece in the next day's paper had made it seem as though his dad had spent his declining years as an old drunk, which was totally untrue.

"Okay, I'll get to the point, Derek. I've heard from several sources now that you had an accident a short while ago, and that ever since, you've had a remarkable sense of smell. Is that right?"

Derek's wariness now transformed into irritation. "Who told you that?" he said.

"Like I said, several sources," the reporter replied. "Of course, I can't say who, exactly, but it is my business to have contacts all over the region. Anyway, to start with, I'd just like you to confirm that it's true – that your sense of smell has become incredibly heightened. Then I'd like to hear some details – and maybe see what you can do. I brought some samples of things with me for you to try to detect from a distance – you know, so I can tell our readers that the whole thing isn't just a hoax."

Derek stared at the man. "What was your name again? he said.

"Rohan," he replied, "Rohan Sinclair."

"Well, it's like this Rohan, I'm a fairly private person, and the last thing I want is my name and personal details being printed in any sort of publication – especially a fucking right-wing, gossip-ridden rag that tries to pass itself off as a newspaper. So no, I'm not going to talk to you about my accident, or about anything else. What I suggest is that you get into your car and take you arse and your little blobs of peanut butter and strawberry jam away from here." *Fuck!* he immediately thought to himself, *Why did I say that?*

"The reporter's eyes widened. He quickly looked back at his car and then again at Derek. "Jesus, was that just a lucky guess, or…or… You really can smell them can't you? What else?" he asked, excited. "Just give me one more."

Derek put his hand on the van door. "Rifkin, you still in there?" he called.

"Now there's no need to be like that, Mister Sadler," the reporter said, reverting to formality as he edged away. "We're going to print something – you may as well make sure that it's accurate." He saw the look on Derek's face, and continued to step backwards towards his car.

At first, Derek wanted to respond with something officious like, 'You print anything that's not true about me, and you'll hear from my lawyer'. But it didn't sit well with him, he wouldn't normally say something like that; and anyway, he didn't actually have a lawyer – not since old Bill Watson had died three years ago. So, instead, he simply said, "Go on, fuckoff, and don't come back."

Sinclair saw Derek pull down on the van's door handle, so he turned and quickly walked to his car, and opened its door. But instead of promptly getting in, he fumbled with the camera around his neck. And before Derek understood what was going on, the reporter had taken two or three photographs in quick succession. Moments later the white car was speeding back to the main road.

Rifkin had been whining at the window so Derek let him out. The dog immediately ran to where the car had been, and after a short sniffing interval, pissed in the depression that one of the back tyres had left in the ground. Derek didn't fully understand the dog's motive for doing this but it seemed like a good idea, so he walked over and did the same.

Back up at the house, Mary was just coming down the stairs, a pile of folders under one arm. Little Harry was behind her; he had a piece of rope tied to his small backpack and was watching it plop down from one step to the other as he tugged on the rope. Derek sat in the van and watched for a moment, smiling. Mary obviously didn't know what was happening behind her, but when she got to the bottom of the stairs and turned around she saw what her youngest was doing. He couldn't hear what she said, but Harry lowered his head and then walked back up the stairs and started to untie the rope. Derek chuckled; it was like watching an old silent comedy flick.

Mary wandered over to the van as Derek was getting out. "You're a bit late aren't you?" she said. It wasn't the least bit accusatory despite the concern she'd been feeling over the last few weeks about her husband's more relaxed approach to his work. She hadn't yet decided whether it was a good thing or not.

"Yeah, well, I've just had an encounter with Rohan-the-Reporter. He…"

"Oh, don't tell me that horrible man waited for you down at the road? What a dick! He tried to weasel his way into waiting in the house. I told him you wouldn't be back for a long while and that you wouldn't be interested in talking to him anyway. He was too insistent and too much of a sleaze for me, so I told him to get off the property – that your accident and its aftermath was no-one's business except your own." And then as an afterthought she added, "I did the right thing, didn't I?"

"Of course you did," Derek replied. "It's what I did too, but he got a couple of pictures with his camera…and I think I blurted out something that probably encouraged him. What I wanna know, though, is how he got wind of what I could do. Who the fuck's been talking to him?"

"Well, it wouldn't have been any of your friends – not intentionally anyway. But you know what reporters are like. It can seem as though they're just having a friendly little chat, when in fact they're really trying to squeeze information out of you."

Derek remembered his father's funeral and the ostensibly sympathetic and interested reporter he'd spoken to. "Yeah I know," he replied.

"Someone at the hospital probably said something too." Mary continued. "I don't mean Barrington or Whatshername but, you know, one of the nurses or aides or whoever."

Derek nodded. He wanted to say more about the

encounter but was being distracted by the sweet, slightly tangy smell of apples. Harry was walking over to his mum, backpack in his hand. Derek gestured with a nod towards the boy, and recalled the incident on the stairs that had just occurred. "He had apples in his bag didn't he?"

Mary sighed…but also grinned. "Yes, four big Red Deliciouses," she said. "I imagine they'll all be turning fairly brown by now.

Early in the morning on the following Friday, the phone started ringing. Apparently Derek had made page five of the *Northern Tribune*.

"Oh, geez, look at it – he's made me sound like a friggin' freak; 'Human Bloodhound In Our Midst'." Derek usually tried to modify his speech when Harry was around, but the article was making him angry. "Bloody journalist; look, he even contacted the hospital trying to get something out of them – just like you said. Mary reached out and touched his arm but then abruptly pulled her hand away as the phone on the wall starting ringing again. "And not that I care," he said as she stood up and walked behind him, "but look at this, he couldn't even spell my name right – Jesus, it was staring him right in the face on the side of the van. Dickhead." Derek pushed the paper away, and Mary answered the phone.

"What's wrong Daddy? Has someone written bad things about you in the newspaper?" Harry had a spoon loaded with cereal in his hand but he lowered it back into the bowl as he stared at his father, worry on his young face. His mother had taken the phone out the back door, but they could still hear her – answering yet another enquiry, probably from family or friends.

"No, they're not bad things, Harry, just stuff I don't want everyone to read about." Seeing his son's expression made Derek less hostile; right now it was more important to allay the little fella's concerns than to vent his anger. "It's not a big thing though – nothing to worry about. By the way, how's that new cereal – any good?"

Despite being only six years old Harry saw straight through his father's diversionary tactic. "It's about your nose isn't it?" And then he grinned as he remembered the term Mary had recently used, "Your 'magic sniffer'."

"Yep, that's right; it's about your good ol' dad's honker," Derek replied, now with a cheery voice, partly forced. "I just wanted it to be kept a bit of a secret, that's all."

"Well, I haven't told anyone at school about how good you are at smelling stuff...and I'm not going to, even if they ask me about it. I'm just gunna say, 'It's none of your business'."

Having made what he clearly thought was a decisive plan of action that would help his dad, Harry began shovelling cereal into his mouth – smiling at Derek and dribbling milk down his chin. Mary re-entered the kitchen just as Tim walked in from the lounge room. "What's going on?" the teenager said. "Why's the phone been ringing all morning?" Derek picked up the newspaper and handed it to his older son.

While Tim was reading, Derek looked at his wife. "Who was that, another one of your cousins?" He grinned, it wasn't meant to be a slight against her family.

"No," she replied. "It was a producer from CQE TV. She wanted to know if the article was correct, and if it was, whether they could come out and do an interview."

"Oh, great. You didn't encourage them did you?"

"I told her that for a while after your accident you thought you could smell things that weren't there, that it's called 'parosmia' and that it's not uncommon in people who suffer certain sorts of head injuries. I said you were over it now – back to normal – and that there was no story; that the article in the paper was not only inaccurate but also way out of date. She seemed to lose interest pretty quickly."

The three males all stared at Mary. Derek had always told his sons that lying was not a good thing to do, and now here was their mother admitting to quite a large one – clearly there'd be a bit of explaining to do…and probably an extended moral debate. But he was glad she'd got rid of the TV people so cleverly – Mary could lie well when she felt she had to. He turned his attention to Tim, and gestured at the newspaper. "That's what all the phone ringing's been about – what do you think of it?"

"Not a bad photo; you can even see Rifkin in the van."

Derek took the paper and examined it. "Hey yeah, I missed that before. Look Harry, Mary, there's the dog in the van."

Later in the day, Derek was standing in the cockpit of a ten-metre yacht that had not stood up well to the rigours of a recent race. It was on the hard in the Ross Harbour Marina. He and Jono had checked out the damage earlier in the week and had carried out a few minor repairs in-between other jobs, but today they intended to work solidly on this boat alone. That's what Derek had said, anyway, but the truth was, he really didn't feel like working right now – the sea breeze was presenting him with some intriguing aromas, and he felt that investigating these would be a much more appealing activity.

"Aww, shit!" Jono cried from somewhere inside the hull near the stern. There'd been a fairly loud bump, and Derek assumed it was his apprentice hitting his head on a deck beam or some other obstruction in the low, narrow compartment in which he was crawling.

"Are you all right?" he called.

There was a pause – just long enough for Derek to feel a tiny prod of concern. Then came a muffled answer. "Yeah…bloody beam."

After some scuffling movements that made the

vessel vibrate slightly in its cradle, Jono appeared in the companionway rubbing one of his temples.

"Givusalook," Derek said as his apprentice stepped up into the cockpit and sat on one of the side thwarts.

"Nah, it's all right – thought I had room to sit up. Bloody torch went out just at the wrong time."

Despite his dissuasiveness, Derek gently pulled the young man's hand away and examined his head. "No cuts, but a bit of a bump." He offered him a handkerchief. "Get some water on this from the galley and put it on your head." Jono looked down at the neatly-folded white cloth. "Go on, take it," Derek said. "I haven't used it."

"No snot?" Jono asked as he took the piece of cloth.

"Oh yeah, like I've had a sinus infection for the last month and that's the only thing I've been blowing my nose on," Derek said with a grin in his voice but not on his face. "In fact, I'm culturing some new bacteria on the mucous, and thinking of offering it to the biological warfare people in the defence department."

"So no snot," Jono repeated as he disappeared back into the boat.

"Not a single fucking micro-boogie's worth," his boss called after him.

A few minutes later, Jono again stepped into the cockpit, now holding the wet handkerchief to the side of his head. "Have you had a look inside the steering pedestal already?" he said as he nodded towards the tall white stand onto which the boat's wheel was attached.

Derek had caught the whiff of some sort of sea creature that he wasn't familiar with out in the bay – maybe a dugong – and his attention was focused on the direction and nature of the odour. He heard Jono's words but they didn't register – made no impact.

"Earth to Derek, Earth to Derek, this is channel sixteen, please reply."

Derek turned to his companion. "What? What did you say?"

"I asked if you'd already taken the top off the pedestal and checked the cable," Jono said, a slightly worried look in his eyes – this had been happening a lot lately.

"The pedestal…oh, no, no, I haven't had a chance. I'll do it in a minute."

Jono had far too much respect for his boss to be critical of his work ethic; Derek was one of the hardest working men he'd ever met, and he was a master of his trade. But ever since the accident Jono had noticed a slow change taking over Derek's behaviour. Increasingly, the man seemed to be off daydreaming rather than concentrating on the job at hand, and he wasn't sure, but it seemed that the quality of Derek's work was also suffering. Although, on this last point, it might've just been that he was leaving more of the finishing work to Jono, himself – doing it on purpose like, as part of his final training. Still, it was a bit unsettling, and Jono wondered whether he should say anything.

"Yeah, well I'll just get the fluorescent tube and go back to where I was," the apprentice said. "I see the owner must've put in that support post for the cracked beam. It's a bit of a messy job but it'll hold okay – probably not worth pulling apart."

"What, on the starboard side, second beam?" Derek said, raising an eyebrow.

"Yeah, that's the one," Jono replied.

"That's mine," Derek said matter-of-factly, "I did it a couple of days ago…when you were over at the yacht club."

For a moment, Jono thought his boss was joking – it wouldn't be unusual. But he quickly saw that this wasn't the case, and he frowned. It was such a crap piece of work – a real amateurish quick-fix: dribbled epoxy, roughly fashioned joins, wooden shims to make up for a wrongly cut length. What was going on with Derek? Was it maybe to do with his accident and the smelling ability that people were now jabbering on about? – although Derek had said nothing to him directly regarding this, and he hadn't asked. Or was there something happening in his private life that was distracting him? The strange thing was, Derek didn't seem to be at all concerned about his apparently changing attitude to work – didn't even seem to notice any change. Jono looked at the older man. There and then he decided to say something. He opened his mouth and was about to speak when another voice – female – rose up from below where they were standing.

"Excuse me, would you be Mister Sadler?"

The two tradesmen looked over the side of the yacht and saw a late twenty-something, short-haired blonde staring up at them. She was wearing a white T-shirt under an open denim shirt, and what looked like a short, pleated black skirt – although the length was hard to tell from where they stood. Derek noticed that she also smelt good – no masking perfume, just pleasant body odour. The overall impression was of a happy and robust woman.

"Yeah, that's me," Derek called down. "Can I help you?"

"Mister Sadler, my name is Amanda Crowther; I'm a film and TV producer. I wonder if I could have a chat with you?"

Suddenly, Derek didn't care how pleasant she smelled. "If it's about the article in today's paper then forget it," he called down. "It was misleading – a mistake – a total stuff-up." He looked across to Jono whose mouth was slightly open – the lad had read the article and, from what he'd been quietly observing, it had seemed credible – maybe even accurate. Derek gave him a quick wink, and softly said "Shhh," under his breath. *Bugger it, here I am lying again*, he thought, surprised at the ease of doing so, but still feeling some guilt.

"Well, can I talk to you about that?" the woman called back.

"Jesus," Derek said quietly. He then looked at Jono. "Just keep on with what you're doing," he said as he flung his leg over the yacht's safety rail and stepped onto the ladder resting against the gunwale. "I'm coming down," he called, "but I can't give you long."

When he was on the ground he saw that she was a pretty woman – her penetrating blue eyes complementing her scent, one that now suggested steadfastness and perseverance. He immediately knew that he wouldn't be able to successfully lie to this woman.

"Mister Sadler, I am part owner of a company called 'Serendipity Productions'. We get most of our income from making short television documentaries and newsbites and interviews that we sell to commercial broadcasters. We're located in Sydney but I'm up here doing some preparatory work for a feature we're making about the drought and its effect on farmers in the region." Derek listened but didn't respond; he was enjoying watching her eyes and smelling her breath. She went on. "Anyway, I read the article about you in today's *Northern Tribune*, and I've spoken to the reporter who wrote it, and I thought it might be worth having a chat with you."

"For what reason?" Derek said, knowing full well what the reason was, but wanting to hear it from her.

She came straight to the point. "I think we could

make a very interesting and saleable documentary about you and your ability, Mister Sadler, and you could make some decent money from the exercise too." She stared at Derek, the hint of a smile at the corners of her mouth. "But you say the article was wrong – a mistake? That's not what Rohan Sinclair at the paper said when I telephoned him – he's the reporter who spoke to you."

"I know who he is, and excuse my French, but he's a sleazy arsehole," Derek replied.

"I know there were probably some inaccuracies in his story – I notice he spelled your name wrongly for instance – but overall, was it more or less correct?"

Derek was impressed but he also felt trapped. If he continued to lie to this Amanda woman then she'd know, and then she'd probably pursue him relentlessly, asking questions of friends, snooping into his private life – just like that fucking journalist – and end up doing the same sort of thing: a cheap, sensationalist-type report over which he had no control. Except this time it would be on everyone's fucking television screen. And he didn't want to lie, anyway; just wanted to be left to himself. But maybe he was being paranoid. Maybe if he simply told her to go away, she would.

"If I told you I didn't want to talk about it with anyone, would you just leave it alone?" he asked, deciding it would be insulting to try to persist with the deception – and fruitless.

She continued to hold him with her eyes. "If you asked me to walk away now, then of course I would," she replied. "But I can tell you, there'll be others who won't be so polite and who have absolutely no scruples about how they get the story they want."

"So what would stop those people coming after me even if I do speak to you?" Derek asked, frowning.

"We'd sign a contract clearly specifying that you will only speak to us about your ability." I'd see that word got around that no one else could touch you – that we had exclusive rights. That'd reduce the hassling considerably." She paused while she watched Derek lean against the cradle and rub a finger across his brow. "Of course all this is hypothetical at this stage," she said. "I don't even know what you can actually do with your sense of smell. So far, I'm treating anything I've read or been told as nothing more than rumour."

Derek sighed. "Well, I can tell that you washed with plain, unscented soap this morning, and that you had bananas and toast for breakfast, with black coffee."

She stared, no hint of a smile now. "Sugar?" she said.

"Can't tell," he replied. "But you've either been sitting on some gum leaves recently, or you've got some in your pocket."

She reached into a pocket in her skirt and pulled out a small sprig of leaves and gumnuts. "I found this under a tree when I was walking around the marina looking for you," she said. "It took my fancy – thought I might stick it in a little vase or something." She nodded her head. "That's pretty amazing." She saw a grin appear on his face, and then mirrored it with one of her own. "So what do you think?" she said. "Might we be able to work together? I know we haven't talked about money but…"

Derek held up his hand. "It's not a question of money," he said. "It's a question of privacy and…I dunno… sensitivity to my situation."

She nodded while still holding him with those eyes. "I think we could work something out that would keep us both happy," she said. "Maybe I could take you to lunch and we could talk about the details."

"I have to tell you now, I'm not signing anything today or making any commitment – not until I've thought about it and talked it over with my wife."

"That's fine with me," she replied. "But I suggest you don't take too long." Derek remained silent, so she continued. "Okay, I'll come and get you at one o'clock; how's that sound?"

He nodded his acceptance, and shook her outstretched hand, and then watched as she walked away. He hoped he was doing the right thing.

It was still only mid afternoon when he turned off the road and up the driveway. He couldn't be bothered going back to the marina, and he'd told Jono what to do on the racing boat – it'd all be okay. Besides, Mary would be home from school by now, and he had a lot to tell her about the lunch meeting.

As he drove up to the house he saw a white holden sedan – the latest model – parked on the grass. *Not another fucking reporter*, he thought as he got out of the van. But then he saw that the car had a government number plate – commonwealth government.

Chapter 6

Mary tried, but she couldn't stifle her giggle. "You want him to what?" she managed to get out.

"Basically, our department would like to see whether your husband could help in the defence of the country," the man in the sunglasses said.

Mary was still grinning. "No, I mean the bit about sniffing out terrorists."

"It was only a hypothetical example," the other man replied. "We don't even know what your husband's capabilities are at this stage – apart from what we've read in the medical report – so our ideas of how he might be useful are fairly vague."

Derek ran his fingers through his hair, and caught a whiff of stale aftershave. What a day it had been. What a week – what a month. He came home wanting to talk to Mary about his discussions with Amanda Crowther, the TV producer – whether to work with her or not was going to be a hard enough decision to make. But that was a minor concern compared with what confronted him now – fucking Bill and Ben the government men (he couldn't remember their real names), and their request that he go to Canberra next week to be 'evaluated' by their colleagues. They were both staring at him now, waiting for a comment. A strange pair: one in a snappy grey suit, short-cropped hair, still wearing his wraparound sunnies even though he was in the lounge room – a real stereotype FBI-style spook; and the other just the opposite: long hair tied back in a ponytail, short-sleeved shirt with a palm-tree print, shorts, sandals – a bit of a backroom boffin type, but pretty senior it appeared. Derek wondered if they got on in private – they looked like they were from different galaxies.

"Let me get this right," he said. "You want me to stop all my work, leave my family, and get on a plane to Canberra this coming Tuesday…in four days time?"

"I thought you'd be honoured, Mister Sadler," Sunglasses said. "To be given the opportunity to serve your country in such a unique way." Derek decided he didn't like this bloke, didn't appreciate being treated like a child. He glanced at Mary, she obviously felt the same.

"Honoured, ay?" Derek replied. Mary waited for the sharp jab that was certain to follow, but the other man – seeming to sense Derek's annoyance – spoke first.

"I understand the hassle it would be for you, Mister

Sadler, you've got a life here that you have to maintain. But you'd only be gone for a week, and the government will pay you for your time – as a consultant – as well as all the travel and accommodation costs, etcetera."

Mary looked across to Derek, and then back at Ponytail. "How much?" she said. "Will he be paid, I mean?"

"Well, you tell me." He looked at Derek. "What would be your consultancy fee for a week's work?"

Derek twisted his mouth. "Aw, I dunno. My hourly boatbuilding rate is usually…"

"Four thousand dollars," Mary interrupted. "That would be a reasonable fee for a week's work don't you think Darling?"

Derek grinned. His wife was brilliant. Now he wouldn't have to get into an argument about his privacy versus the possible good of the nation or any other bullshit like that – the decision to cancel would be simply based on economics; he wanted far more than the government would be prepared to pay. He winked at Mary.

"Okay, that sounds fair enough," Ponytail said.

Derek's expression suddenly changed, his moment of smugness gone. "Won't you have to ask someone higher up the ladder?" he said, "and, you know, fill in forms and meet with a committee – it's a lot of money for a single week."

"No, I'm in charge of the unit that will be working with you, Mister Sadler. I don't have to ask anyone. And like I said, the amount sounds fair enough."

Derek could see that Sunglasses didn't think it was fair enough – his disapproval was obvious from his expression: rolled together lips, big exhalation through his nose, turning his head away; you could almost see his thought bubble: *why the hell should this guy get three times the amount I'm getting paid – he's just a boatbuilder for fuck's sake.*

Clearly, Mary was as stunned as her husband; she looked at him and raised her eyebrows and shoulders in a 'I-don't-know,-it's-up-to-you' gesture.

"No needles, electrodes, probes, drugs or anything like that," Derek said.

"Nothing at all of that nature," Ponytail replied. "We just want to see what you can detect in different circumstances, and the accuracy of your assertions. Then, depending on the results, we'd like to discuss how you might work with a number of government agencies in the future. But no intrusive testing – my group isn't interested in the hows and whys of what you can do, only in your actual capabilities."

"And tell me again how you got to see the medical report about me," Derek said. "I thought that sort of thing was private."

The man looked down at his sandals. "Normally such things would be totally confidential, Mister Sadler but… I really can't say any more than I already have; just that some otherwise-restricted information is passed on to me because of the work I'm involved in."

Derek glanced across at Mary. "Bloody doctors – I'd rather trust a fox in a chook pen." He then took in a deep breath and slowly blew it out through his mouth. "Okay," he said. "Put it in writing and sign it – including the payment part – and I'll do it." Again, he looked at Mary, this time hoping for an expression of approval. She smiled, but there was concern there too. Ponytail nodded his approval and reached for the laptop case sitting on the floor next to him.

At that point, everyone heard the banging of the kitchen door, and a moment later Rifkin walked into the room. The dog looked at each of the two strangers, and then wandered over to Derek and dropped a giant, dead grasshopper at his feet. He sat for a moment while his owner picked up the crushed insect and examined it. The others didn't know of course, but Derek's examination was performed more with his nose than his eyes – an interesting smell, like cut grass and bile and soil all mixed together. Rifkin then stood up and sauntered out of the room. Derek wasn't really thinking when he too raised himself from the sofa and followed his dog.

"Derek?" Mary said as he walked past her.

He turned. "Oh, umm, I'll just be a minute – something I have to check outside," he said.

The two other men stared at each other while Mary

maintained her sad smile. "Okay, Darling," she said. "Don't be long."

Stepping out through the huge sliding glass doors of the terminal, and into the natural, untreated air of Canberra was – as far as Derek was concerned – like suddenly taking all your clothes off while wandering around the South Pole. "Jesus, it's fucking cold here – how can you stand it?" he said to the young man who had met him at the arrivals area.

"You get used to it," the youth replied – deadpan, neither friendly nor unfriendly. He pointed to a car parked a short way off, and Derek followed him, pulling the wheeled suitcase that he'd bought at Crazy Clark's in Yuragan. His young guide had tried to take it for him but Derek had insisted on carrying his own luggage – he wasn't going to allow himself to be treated like fucking royalty, it wasn't his style; he was just a simple working man for Christ's sake.

Another man, the driver of the white sedan, was more forceful. He popped the boot, and got out from behind the steering wheel as the other two approached. He then greeted Derek, and literally grabbed the suitcase from his hands, lifting it into the boot in a smooth and obviously well-practised action. Derek clutched onto his shoulder bag, making it clear that *it* was going to stay with him. Not that it really mattered, but he didn't feel comfortable with this sort of treatment. He might be a visitor here but that didn't mean he was going to give up control of what happened to him, not even at this simple level. Let go here and the next thing you know he'd be doing whatever else the Canberra gang expected of him.

The truth was, he was a bit frightened by the whole exercise. Sure, he'd only be here for a week, and he'd be making a nice packet of money for doing what might in fact be a bit of fun. But this was a world of bureaucracy and politics: where actions and words didn't mean what they at first appeared to mean, and where people fought for territories that he knew nothing about. He'd been here years ago just after finishing school – stayed with his Uncle Freddy and got a part-time job in the Immigration Department, doing lowly clerical stuff. His dad had wanted him to have a chance at a different lifestyle. But he'd hated it – only stayed for five months, and then went back to Yuragan to be apprenticed to his old man. It was one of the best decisions he'd ever made. Canberra had sucked then, and it probably sucked even more now.

Their first stop was the motel room that had been booked for Derek. They spent only ten minutes there, registering him and dropping off his luggage, and then another ten minutes driving to the building where his first official meeting was to take place. During this short journey, the young man sat next to the driver and said almost nothing to Derek. He gave the impression that he thought this little errand was beneath him – that picking up some yobbo who obviously wasn't a senior public servant or anyone else of importance, was a job that should have been given to a person much lower in the pecking order.

The building they arrived at turned out to be a large, white concrete box with windows – large in that it covered a huge area; in terms of height, it was actually quite modest, rising to only five or six storeys. Derek and his guide were driven right up to the main entrance – a simple arrangement of two rotating glass doors set in an otherwise unremarkable concrete wall, a roof extending out over the driveway. 'The John Monash Building' was spelled out in dull, brown metal letters above the doors. Derek walked up the few steps from the car, and then stood, looking up at the name.

"He was a general in the First World War," his guide said with a touch of disdain. "General Sir John to be exact."

"Yes, I know," Derek replied. "I was wondering whether it was silicon bronze or aluminium bronze that's been used for the letters; do you know?"

The young man stared at him, uncertain whether his charge was taking the piss or not. "I've no idea," he replied.

Derek nodded his head and continued walking.

Getting beyond the reception area took more time than the drive from the motel. Derek had been forewarned about the rigmarole that would occur, and had brought his driver's licence, birth certificate extract, and credit card to help confirm his ID. Two men in uniform escorted him into a small side room and took his fingerprints and several photographs. When he emerged from the room, his sullen young guide was gone but there at the desk was Ponytail – who he now knew as Pierce Lamuir, the head of the multi-departmental task force whose job it was to 'explore innovative national security safeguards'; or something like that, Derek couldn't remember his exact words.

"Good to see you Derek," Pierce said as he picked up a clipboard. "Just let me put my signature on this identity confirmation form, and then I'll take you up to the third floor where we'll be meeting and doing a bit of preliminary work."

The only way to leave the reception area – besides going back out the front entrance – was to pass through one of the several sliding doors that apparently led to the lifts and to other sections of the building. Each of these doors had a uniformed (and armed) guard next to it, and to get through, you had to show him an ID card like the one Derek was now wearing – clipped to the top pocket of his jacket. "It gets worse the further you go into the bowels of the place," Pierce said as he turned to Derek.

"Same with mine," Derek replied as he lifted his plastic image towards the guard's face – trying to be helpful.

At a second checkpoint up on the third floor, Derek had to be actually signed in as a 'special consultant'. There was a guard here too, and as Pierce finished scribbling his signature, the guard said, "Thank you Doctor Lamuir."

A few seconds later, while walking down a corridor, Derek could feel the annoyance rising in his psyche – he was beginning to sense that maybe he'd been duped. "So you're another bloody doctor, are you? I didn't know that."

"Not a medical doctor," his host replied quickly, seeming to understand his guest's concern. "I've got a PhD in chemistry."

"Oh," Derek replied, his anxiety level dropping back to normal.

"…and one in politics," Pierce went on.

"My wife would call you a 'real doctor'," Derek said. "A 'double real doctor', maybe."

"And what about you?" Pierce asked with a grin.

"Dunno; I had enough fucking trouble remembering your first name." They both laughed.

The meeting took place in a modest sized room that Pierce said was often used for presentations. There was a pull-down screen at one end, together with a large whiteboard and an overhead projector. A series of small tables had been pushed together to form a big committee-meeting type table, and around this sat eight or so people, together with Pierce and Derek. Pierce had introduced each of the others – most were representatives of various departments – and Derek had promptly forgotten who was who. Their scents, however, remained with him – in his memory. Just as most people would identify individuals in a group by visual characteristics – the lady with the big mole on her chin, the guy with the shaved head, the brunette with the big knockers – he was immediately able to perceive the distinctive signature and overlay smells of each person as they were introduced.

Of course, all their smells were in the room together, mixing and swirling and drifting apart, but that didn't seem to confound Derek at all – being able to focus on the scent of a particular person, and to briefly analyse many of its components, was almost as natural to him as doing the same thing visually. In fact, when he'd thought about this a few nights ago, he wasn't sure whether he was now using his eyes as much as he used to for examining and identifying things. Was he carrying on as normal in this regard, with his heightened sense of smell simply adding to an already sharp visual awareness of the world? Or was he losing some of his sight-related powers of perception because of his osmatic acuity – as though you could never be in credit, only maintain the balance you had; like that physics law he had learned at school about the conservation of energy. Whatever the answer was, it didn't really bother him; he now adored having his unique ability, glorified in it. It was so immediate and interesting and stimulating.

His previous qualms were now all but gone.

Actually, he'd been surprised that such a deep philosophic idea had crossed his mind. Few such thoughts seemed to present themselves to him anymore. If *anything* was disappearing from his mental landscape, it was the amount of time he spent reflecting and contemplating. He was sure the ability was still there, but just not the urge – his sense of smell and the immediacy of its call on his brain seemed to leave little time for other sorts of thinking. This apparent loss bothered him sometimes, but his concern was always short-lived, always dismissed by a new smell and the images and suggestions that it conjured up.

Pierce told those sitting around the composite table what the purpose of the meeting was – "To get a feel for Mister Sadler's capabilities, and to then determine if, and how, he might be able to contribute to various national security functions."

Of course, everyone would've already been fully aware of why they were there, so Derek assumed that all the introductory stuff was mainly for his benefit, to make him feel comfortable. Any sense of being at ease quickly disappeared, however, when Pierce asked him to give a brief account of what had happened to him, from the moment of the accident to the present. The last time Derek had addressed a group of strangers was when he was the backup best man at Mick O'Rourke's second wedding nine years ago, and he'd been well fortified with booze on that occasion. Still, Pierce encouraged him, and when the others started asking questions, thereby giving him a lead on what to say, he began to loosen up. Forty minutes later he was finished, his story – in general terms – told.

"Okay, so let's move on to a practical demonstration of what Mister Sadler has been talking about," Pierce said. "I've already seen some examples of what he is capable of – when I visited his home last week. But while I was away, Samantha here..." he nodded towards a solid, middle-aged woman wearing rimless glasses, "...coordinated the setting up of a series of...let us call them 'situations' that were designed as a result of my discussions with each of you and your departmental groups."

While he'd been talking, Solid Sam and another woman had been placing little carved wooden boxes – about ten of them – equally spaced along the centre of the big table. "Mister Sadler," the other woman said, "have you ever smelled heroin?"

"I didn't think it had a smell – you know, in its pure form. And please...and this goes for all of you," he said looking around at the others, "forget the Mister Sadler stuff – just call me Derek."

"Well yes, that is probably correct," the woman replied. "I say 'probably' because some authorities still argue that even the pure form has a very slight odour. However, my department usually encounters something less than the pure form – still highly refined but not exactly one hundred percent purity." She reached into her jacket pocket and pulled out a small metal tube with a screw top. She then handed it to Derek. "Here, smell this," she said. "It's a sample from a large shipment that we recently intercepted."

Derek took the container and while doing so, noticed the words 'Janine' and 'Customs' written on a stick-on tag on the woman's lapel – he looked around and saw that everyone else was wearing a similar tag; he was surprised, he'd not noticed this previously.

Even before removing the top from the tube he was aware of a strange odour associated with it – not the oily human scents that were clearly caused by the different people who had handled it, but something quite different. Describing its characteristics to others would be nigh on impossible, but it bore a resemblance to some vitamin pills he remembered taking at one time – with the slightest hint of vinegar, and something less pleasant, like…stale cat piss. When he did get the top off, the smell seemed to suddenly burst in his head – so much stronger, and definitely unpleasant. He looked down at the slightly off-white powder lying inside the tube, shook it around a bit, and then promptly screwed the lid back on.

"Don't you want to see if you can detect any odour," Janine of Customs said, obviously surprised that he hadn't stuck the tube under his nose and taken a whiff. "I couldn't smell anything, and neither could my colleagues, but I thought…" She trailed off, a mix of disappointment and mild annoyance in her voice.

"I don't want to get my nostrils too close, now do I?" Derek replied. A few of the others chuckled, but the Customs lady just glared at him. "Don't worry," he said, "I think I've got the scent pretty well tagged already."

"Yes, well why don't we see about that," she replied tartly. "On the table you can see ten small, wooden boxes. I would like you to tell us if any of them contain the same sort of heroin." She smiled but it was the smile of someone who enjoyed witnessing failure in others. Derek decided he didn't like Janine of Customs – didn't like her smell either. Then Pierce spoke.

"Maybe we could all pull our chairs back to the walls so Mister Sadler…Derek…can more easily move around the table while doing his examination." Everyone immediately followed the suggestion – except Derek himself who remained in his chair.

Silence descended on the gathering as all the others watched him, waiting for him to go through some uncertain process of evaluation. Would he pick up each box in turn and pass it under his nose? Would he shake each one first? Would he need the lights turned off – to avoid any interfering visual stimulation? Would he directly compare pairs of boxes – one in each hand, sniffing one and then the other, until he finally homed in on those containing the narcotic?

As it turned out, he simply pushed his chair back a little, looked back and forth along the table's length, and then looked up at Janine who was standing with a few others at the wall across from the table. "They've all had heroin in them at some time recently, but that one at the end and that fourth one," he pointed, "they've got the stuff in them right now." The woman had her mouth open, and her eyes were big; everyone was looking at her. But Derek hadn't finished. "All the others have talcum powder in them – not perfumed thank God – except that one up the other end which has something else, I think it's castor sugar or something like that."

Janine appeared dazed – not disbelieving or incredulous; simply dazed. "So is he right, Janine?" one of the others – a tall man – asked?

"What? Ahmm, I er…don't know. I mean I have to check each of the boxes myself." She walked over to one end of the table, and picked up the first one. While she was doing this, Pierce spoke.

"Remember, we agreed to use a double-blind protocol for these sorts of…situations – so none of us could possibly give cues about which container held the target substance or item." People murmured and nodded.

Janine opened the hinged lid of the first box and showed everybody what was inside – nothing – the box appeared to be empty. However, she then produced a small screwdriver from her briefcase and stuck its blade into the box, in the fine gap between one of the ends and the bottom. After a bit of twisting and levering she popped out a small rectangle of wood – it was a false bottom. Underneath was a sealed plastic bag the same size as the bottom and filled to a thickness of a few millimetres with off-white powder. The bag had a big, black 'H' marked on it.

Ten minutes later, everyone was back sitting around the table – the boxes were still in their original order but each now had its plastic-bagged contents lying next to it. "So how were you able to do that without picking up each box, or even just getting close to each one?" Janine said. "Smells can't be that directional – all the molecules must mix together."

"Really?" Derek replied, not pleased with her implication that he must have used something other than his sense of smell to identify the contents.

"Well it stands to reason, doesn't it? Not even our best sniffer dogs could distinguish between these boxes without examining each one individually."

"Oh, is that right?" Derek replied. "And how did you work that out – did you ask them?"

Janine frowned. She was supposed to be the one doing the attacking here. "What do you mean?" she said.

"What I mean is… Look, it doesn't matter how I do it

– I don't know how I do it. All I know is that I can usually identify the source of a smell without necessarily having to get right up next to it – mixing molecules or not."

"Janine, I'm not sure what the problem is." It was the tall man speaking. "Derek just passed this test… situation, sorry…with one-hundred percent accuracy. It's extraordinary."

She swung her head around and glared across at the man. "Not exactly a hundred percent," she said. "It was icing sugar in the last box, not castor sugar."

"Oh, Jesus," Derek said as he turned to Pierce, and under the cover of laughter and chatter from some of the others he whispered, "What the fuck's got up her?"

"Nothing…for quite a long time, I suspect," Pierce whispered back.

The rest of the day remained pretty much the same. Different little tests, which Pierce still insisted on calling 'situations', were given to Derek. Besides a variety of drugs, he was able to identify a range of explosives, and a sample of small animals – both native and exotic – that were brought into the room briefly by special handlers (who were then directed to wait outside). He wasn't very good at distinguishing between new handguns and other small, metal, mechanical devices, but if they'd been fired then he could spot them easily – the oxidised chemicals from the bullet charges being a dead giveaway.

One result that caused a lot of interest with the tall man and several others was when Derek was able to determine who, in the group, had recently handled sample documents – even after they'd been wiped with a dry cloth to remove actual fingerprints. It was during this test that Derek suddenly had a vision of himself in court, appearing as an 'expert' for some government agency, and having to behave like a performing dog for the jury just to verify the accuracy of his advanced hyperosmia. He'd already become a bit weary from all the testing, but this little fantasy had made him shudder. There was no way he was going to be a courtroom performer, *no fucking way*.

The original onslaught from bitchy-boots of Customs hadn't left him in a good mood either. She had been smart enough to leave him alone for the rest of the day. But her lack of contribution to the rest of the proceedings was just as noticeable as had been her earlier loudmouth scepticism, and he found this a bit unnerving. Who in their right mind likes having a sullen, albeit silent, critic sitting just across from you for six or so hours.

During lunch, Pierce had quietly intimated that she had been highly critical of proceeding with 'such a nonsense project' from the beginning, and that she had a reputation as a bully. "I don't like bullies," Derek had said. "Not one bit."

Now he was in his motel room, lying back on the double bed, and looking up at the ceiling. Already he missed Mary and the kids; and his workshop, his friends, the boats, the town, the bush...Rifkin. The air conditioner buzzed as it attempted to warm the room, and one of the brightly patterned curtains swayed in the artificial breeze. He looked across at the electric kettle sitting on a shelf next to the TV. There were two cups close by, one of them containing sachets of instant coffee and tea-bags, the other packed with paper tubes filled with sugar; the milk would be in the small fridge that was neatly set into the wood-veneer cabinet. It was all very convenient and functional – like moderate quality motels all over the world. But he was becoming depressed. *What a fucking dump,* he thought.

He had just decided to telephone home when there was a knock on the door. He swung his legs off the bed and walked to the end of the room; he expected it would be one of the motel workers checking on something or other – maybe the dripping tap in the bathroom. But when he pulled open the door he was confronted by Pierce. "G'day, Pierce," he said. "I thought you had a dinner to go to – what are you doin' here?"

His visitor blinked as the warm air from the room swept over his face. "Oh, I cancelled it – felt guilty about leaving you here by yourself." He blinked again. "My God, are you thinking of smelting metal in there?"

Derek smiled, and started to feel better. "Hey Double Doc, I'm from a place where your balls don't turn to icicles every time the sun goes down."

Pierce took a step back. "Well, go and give your testicles a quick blast with the bathroom hair dryer, and then get your coat. I'll take you somewhere to eat that I promise will keep you warm."

'Bombay Heaven' was one of a dozen or so Indian restaurants in the ACT. It wasn't located in Canberra City but in the nearby suburb of Belconnen, where government workers live comfortably in middle-class type houses that have grassy front and back yards where dogs bark and children play. Plazas and malls are well established near all the residential areas that feed Canberra, but there are still some small, suburban 'shopping centres' battling away against the giants – little clusters of retail outlets: a newsagency, a butcher, a bakery, a supermarket; and restaurants – lots of restaurants. It was in such a cluster that the Bombay Heaven was situated – between an optometrist's and a video library. It wasn't particularly fancy but the careful placement of large urns and folding wooden screens broke up the floor area and, together with the low lighting, gave the place a relaxed ambience.

"Jesus, this has to be the hottest fucking food I've ever eaten," Derek said as he dipped a torn off piece of naan into the cooling mix of yoghurt and cucumber. "But man, do I like it."

"And remember, you're only eating the very mild version," Pierce said, smiling.

"I know, I know. What did the waiter bloke say the hottest one was, Vindaloon or something. Jesus, if it didn't burn your guts out on the spot then your arse would be in flames the next morning."

Pierce chuckled as he watched Derek take more of the spicy chunks of chicken and lamb and vegetables from the shiny serving bowls. "What about the smell, Derek, what effect does that have on you?"

Derek didn't answer straight away – first finishing the mouthful he was chewing, and then taking a swig from the stubbie of Crown Lager next to his plate. When he'd finished, he leant back in his chair and regarded his host – and the pretty young blonde sitting behind him at the next table. "I know I don't have to tell you that taste and smell are connected," he said. "I'm sure you know a lot more about that than me." Pierce shrugged. "You know, you think you're just tasting something when in fact it's both taste and smell that are combining to give the overall effect. You'd only have to pinch your nostrils together while eating this curry to see what a small contribution your taste buds are making." He stopped for a moment. Just beyond Pierce, the blonde girl's companion had leaned forward and was in the act of planting a big wet one on her lips. Pierce followed Derek's gaze and turned around to see what was going on. He turned back with no change of expression – normal behaviour for a restaurant with an intimate atmosphere like this.

"Anyway," Derek continued, "for me, it's not been like you might think."

"How do you mean?"

"Well, just after the accident, when my sense of smell was having its own private fucking revolution – I mean it was wild, like suddenly getting X-ray vision or being able to hear ants walking – well, the way foods tasted was certainly different, more…you know, enhanced; and usually much, much better. But I seemed to get used to the experience quickly. Like, I dunno, the first piece of pawpaw I ate after the accident was a fantastic experience – totally new, with shades and depths of taste or smell or, you know, the whole package, like I'd never known before. The next piece was good too, but not as impressive – not as explosive. And after a short time of regular pawpaw eating it became nothing overly special. I think it's…"

He trailed off as the couple behind Pierce again grabbed his attention. This time the blonde had leant forward over the narrow table and was kissing the man. One of her hands had started at the side of his face but was now sliding around to the back of his head, pulling his lips harder against hers. Pierce turned but this time didn't immediately turn back. The woman was wearing a low-cut blouse that exposed her shoulders as well as a fair amount of her chest, and the man now had his hands gripped onto her bare, upper arms and either he or she or both were gently rocking her shoulders. Her chest was beginning to heave, and Derek became keenly aware of her feminine secretions. He leaned towards Pierce. "Jesus, if they go much further this place'll get an R-rating," he whispered.

Pierce was in the process of turning back, when another man – older, and wearing an overcoat – came striding towards them from the front of the building. He had Hell in his eyes. "You fucking bitch! You fucking bastard!" he yelled, and he reached into his coat. At this point, he was almost next to Derek's and Pierce's table.

Derek suddenly jumped from his seat and threw himself at the man, grabbed him from behind, and used his substantial strength to pin the guy's arms to his side. There was no micro-planning or weighing up of options or any other sort of higher-order thinking involved in Derek's action. He'd seen and heard exactly the same as the other people sitting nearby, but he'd also been aware of something else, and it was this that prompted him to do what he did.

The man was struggling, but he wasn't very strong, and Derek's hold was like that of a pair of vise-grips – he could make it tighter too, if he wanted – lift the guy off the ground, squeeze him hard, make him pass out; he'd done it before. "Let it go mate," he said quietly in the man's ear. "You know what I'm talking about; let it go...now!" he ended more forcefully.

"I have, I have," the man cried – like really cried, tears beginning to well up in his eyes.

By this time the blonde was on her feet, but still standing back from the commotion. "Leave him alone," she yelled at Derek. "You're hurting him."

Derek glanced around. Two skinny waiters were standing close-by, uncertain what to do. A heftier man – a chef – was striding out of the kitchen. Looks of fear and disbelief were on the faces of other customers. "Pierce, he's got a gun," Derek said to his eating partner who was already standing but, like everyone else, wasn't sure what to do. "Here, inside left pocket, take the fucking thing off him."

To his credit, Pierce acted immediately, didn't ask any questions. He stepped in front of the man – who by now had gone quite limp – and, when Derek nodded and pulled both of the man's arms sideways, away from his body, reached into his overcoat and gingerly pulled out a small pistol. At the sight of this, a woman screamed, and the staff who had been closing in on the pair now promptly stepped back. The blonde fell back in her chair with her hand over her mouth, and then looked down to see her lover boy hiding under the table.

"Shit! Is this thing cocked?" Pierce said as he held the handle of the weapon between his thumb and forefinger, its barrel pointing obliquely to the floor.

"I don't know, just put it on the chair," Derek said.

"And you, mate; you sit on the floor, and don't fucking move or you'll get my knee in your face." The man was now blubbering about being sorry, and he slid down to the floor.

Derek looked around. There was still bewilderment on most faces, but some were already showing smiles, and then someone started to clap, and within seconds the whole restaurant was cheering. While this was happening, an Indian-looking man in a dark suit came up to Derek and shook his hand. Derek didn't catch his name but gathered that he was the owner. With a singsong accent this man suggested that they escort the attacker into the kitchen, "So the other diners can continue their meals without the embarrassment of a criminal sitting on the floor."

Derek beckoned to the big chef, and together they helped the attacker to his feet. The man was now just sniffing back remnant tears. He seemed harmless enough, but Derek still pushed one of his arms up his back – not too hard – and said to the chef, "Here you take him like this, and don't leave him until the cops come." As they walked off towards the kitchen, Derek turned to the owner. "And I suggest you take the gun, and keep it in a safe place." He walked over to where it lay on the table. "Fuck me," he said, looking down. "The fucking safety is off – that bastard really intended to use it." He reached down and clicked the tiny lever into its safety position, and then handed the weapon to the owner who wrapped it in a serviette.

"Thank you my kind sir," the owner said. "Please allow me to come and thank you more fully after the police have been – and," he said, just before walking away, "your meal is on the house, of course – anything you want."

Derek lifted up his fallen chair and sat down. Pierce came and joined him.

"My God Derek, I've never seen anything like that!" Pierce said. "My heart is still thumping somewhere up in my neck." Derek forced a smile and reached for his beer; his hand was shaking. "It was an amazing thing you did, but how did you know the guy had a gun? I saw him put his hand in his coat, but it didn't occur to me that he might be about to pull out a weapon."

Derek guzzled several mouthfuls from the vibrating stubbie, and then looked at his colleague. "You know that test you put me through today – the one with hidden handguns?"

Pierce's eyes widened with sudden understanding. "Where you were only aware of the ones that had been recently fired?" he said.

Derek reached for the stubbie again. "That guy had been practicing," he said. "Clear as a bell."

"Well fuck me," Pierce replied, as an astonished smile spread across his face.

Derek raised his eyebrows and laughed. "Not tonight Josephine," he said as he took another swig.

Chapter 7

Derek stretched his legs out towards the veranda rail. For the umpteenth time he noticed the neatly framed netting that extended from just under the top of the rail down to the floorboards. He'd set this up some time ago when Harry was still a baby – after the little fella had squeezed himself between two of the thin uprights and had almost dropped the four metres to the ground. It was one of those small structural legacies of early parenthood that were no longer necessary but that you kept anyway, like sand pits and rope-and-tyre swings – perhaps in anticipation of future grandchildren. He took a deep breath. There was still a faint aroma associated with the netting, and it brought back razor-sharp memories of those times only a handful of years ago. He remembered all the screwing he and Mary had put themselves through in order to make little Harry. It had been tiring, but not a hardship – no way; he remembered the period with great fondness. He turned his head to Mary. She still looked great, and smelled even better.

"Well?" she asked.

"Huh?"

"You haven't heard a word I've said, have you?"

"Yeah I have," he replied, still smiling; he loved it when she pouted her lips that way. "You were asking about… you know…whether I felt like going to bed with you – like right now."

"Derek," she replied in an irritated tone.

"Sorry Darling, I was off with the fairies again," he replied "…but thinking about you."

"You're hopeless, Derek," she said, trying to appear angry but unable to stop her mouth from grinning. "I asked what the next step is going to be with your government friends."

The question brought Derek back from his light-headed state. "Hey, they're not my friends, Mary," he replied, frowning. "The only bloke worth more than two bob is Pierce. I mean, I wouldn't have even stayed on in Canberra if he hadn't been running things – there were some real arseholes there, you know."

"Alright, bad choice of word," Mary conceded, "but what's the next step, anyway?"

"Well, on Friday, after they'd made me do all those fucking circus tricks earlier in the week, we had this brainstorming session about how I might be useful to them. Some of the suggestions had been pretty obvious from the beginning – like sniffing out drugs and explosives and the rest – but this session was for…what did Pierce call them?…more *esoteric* ideas." He smiled at Mary, proud that he'd remembered the word.

"Very good," she said, mentally reminding herself of what a lovable little boy her husband could still be, sometimes.

"At that stage," he went on, "I just wanted to get out of the place and back to here, so I didn't really suggest anything – just left it to others to come up with ideas. And some were real doozeys: like sending me to a city of a million people with the objective of tracking down a guy after being given an old fucking turban of his, or whatever, to smell."

"Oh, delightful," Mary said. "Still, probably better than old underpants."

"Yeah, but can you imagine it? Jesus, I'm not fucking Superman. One other guy even suggested I get inoculated against all known biological warfare agents and then be trained to detect the odour of the different spores and bacteria and other shit that gets sprayed into the air when the weapons are used."

Mary wrinkled her forehead. "But that wouldn't…"

"Most of them were bullshit ideas, Sweetheart, but, you know, Pierce said anything could be suggested – whether they could possibly work or not would be sorted out later – by him and his select team…and me."

"So when's that going to happen?"

"Well, they were going over the suggestions – and all the circus trick results – even before I got on the plane. And I know they intended to keep at it – right through this weekend. These guys are keen, I tell you. There's obviously some big brownie points to be scored." He sighed. "After that – when they've got a list of what they consider might be feasible, and it's all, you know, prioritized – Pierce'll get in touch with me, and I'll tell him what I think."

"What you think is possible, or what you think you'd be prepared to do?"

He sniffed the morning air – and detected a wombat down in the gully. "Both," he said. "Although, I reckon Pierce…he really is a nice guy, you know. But I'm sure he thinks I'm just gunna tell him how I feel about the ideas – whether they might work or not – and then automatically move onto the next phase of the project; which is to see if some of these things can actually be done. I don't think it's crossed his mind that I might not want to do any of it – even if it's easy for me. I mean, almost everyone there seemed to assume that I'd be over the fucking moon with happiness to do their stupid, human bloodhound jobs. …But I'm not sure I want to."

"Then don't," Mary said with a firm nod of her head. "You owe those people nothing. Don't let them pressure you into something you don't want to do."

"Yeah, well…I'd rather be doing other things – and

be back here with you and the kids…but then I think, if I've got this ability, shouldn't I be using it in a worthwhile way…you know, like helping to protect the country."

"Hey," Mary said, "most of us have the ability to be soldiers or police or other protectors of the nation, but we don't all go and join up, do we? We can be just as useful to society by doing other things besides standing at the frontline."

Derek nodded thoughtfully, but he wasn't entirely convinced. "Pierce and I met privately just before I left Canberra," he said. "He told me in, you know, confidence, that he thought one of the highest priorities might be for me to be a specialist on weapons inspection teams – ones looking for the ingredients of chemical warfare agents. There were an awful lot of components that I was able to quickly learn the odours of and to then detect – even when they were sealed and hidden."

"Sounds dangerous," Mary said, a worried look on her face. She could see that her husband was seriously considering being involved in such an activity despite his uncertainties.

"Oh, I don't know. It's dangerous being a boatbuilder," he replied.

"And you'd be away from here for big stretches of time, I imagine."

He sniffed, that wombat down in the gully had been joined by at least one other. "Yeah, I suppose that's true," he replied, finding it difficult to concentrate on the conversation in the face of what his nose was detecting out in the bush. He started to get up from his seat. "I'm just going to get Rifkin and go for a walk," he said, and then made a squeaking sound with his lips – his way of calling the dog if he was close-by.

Normally, on an occasion like this, Mary would behave sympathetically. She could tell when her husband had detected a scent that he felt compelled to investigate, and knew that his relationship with his dog had been elevated to a different level because of it. Letting them go off together, unhindered, was the best thing to do – otherwise he would become frustrated and preoccupied and be totally useless. But, right now – despite the likely side effects – remaining here and talking was more important. "Just stay put for a couple of minutes will you please, Derek?" she said. "We really need to talk about a couple of other things – your business, being one of them."

Derek groaned as he fell back onto the canvas-and-wood chair. The bush smells called – there was something going on with the wombats. Rifkin had scurried across the floor from elsewhere in the house and was now standing next to his owner, head cocked to one side expectantly.

Mary pulled her chair around so that she now faced Derek, close. As soon as she began to talk, Rifkin sat down (human stuff, it always takes time). "Darling, last week while you were away, I had no less than ten phone calls from people who you had made work agreements with – some of them from more than a month ago. They were all complaining about you either not completing work that you'd started, or about you not even making a start despite lots of promises. None of them even knew you'd be unavailable for a week. It was embarrassing, because I've never heard of anyone complaining about you in this way – not in any way. You've always been so fastidious about getting on with jobs and finishing them promptly."

"Yeah, and never having time to do anything else," he replied as he bowed his head and ran his fingers through his hair.

"Don't get me wrong, Darling," she said, "the kids and I love having you around more – last week aside – and you really were doing too much for too little before the accident, but I'm worried that you might be…I don't know…letting go more than you should." She reached out and touched Derek's knee. "Jono is worried too."

He suddenly looked up. "Jono? What do you mean? Have you two been talking? What the fuck's he been saying?"

"Don't be angry. The boy is concerned about someone he cares for – you," she said. "He came around to see me last Wednesday." She took a breath; Derek could see she was choosing her words. "Derek, you know how much Jono respects you. One of the reasons he's stayed with you for the last four years is because he thinks you are a lot more than just a good tradesman – he considers you a craftsman and an artist, someone he feels privileged to learn from. And he loves working with you – you're his role model for goodness sake."

Derek felt embarrassed hearing this – he knew it was true, but it wasn't something he'd ever actually thought about head-on. "Yeah, I know," he said. "I like Jono too; he's a smart lad, and he'll be a fine boatbuilder."

"Anyway, he was reluctant to say anything about you – I had to draw it out of him – but I'm sure it was the reason he'd come around in the first place." She looked intently at her husband. "He said he could see that you weren't working to your usual standard, not taking the care for detail that has always characterized your work." She paused before continuing. "And that you didn't seem to be bothered about keeping things on schedule any more. One of the callers was the man who you'd given the quote to for building that little cruising catamaran. He said he hadn't heard from you for weeks despite him leaving heaps of messages. He seemed pretty annoyed, and said the deal would be off if you didn't get in touch soon. I thought you really wanted to build that boat."

Derek gently fingered one of his eyebrows, and then gazed off into the distance. "Yeah, well, I did, but..." a crow cawed as it flew overhead and then circled over the gully. Derek smelled blood and a flood of other scents; Rifkin stood up, he could smell them too. "Things have changed," he said as he got to his feet. "You know that. All that stuff about work ethic and quality and care…I just find it hard to concentrate and to plan…I just can't; not any more – there's so much else that catches my attention now." He got to his feet; two more crows were circling and there was now the unmistakable scent of a cat coming from near the creek – what was going on down there? "I really want to go, Mary – we can talk more about this later." He took several steps; Rifkin barked with excitement.

Mary quickly stood up and caught hold of his arm. "Derek, I know you want to go running off into the bush, that your head is probably swimming with sensations and perceptions that I will never understand, but I think you're going to have to find some way of controlling these urges more strongly – otherwise it could end up ruining your life."

He glanced down at her hand on his arm – she had never done this before. She was obviously deeply worried, but he couldn't really see why – his life was fine; every minute was full of wonderful scents and smells: osmatic images, things to investigate. How could anyone think about planning and working and driving themselves to the limit when there was just so much to simply take in from the surroundings? But he knew he'd have to find some sort of balance, blend some part of the old Derek with the version that was still emerging. "I promise I'll work on it, Darling, I really will."

"Then start now," she said. Don't go running off into the bush. Get in the van and drive down to the yacht club or the marina. Walk around, look at the boats, check them out – think of one thing that you might do to each of them to improve it; like you used to do in the old days. See if you can recapture the thrill of being a boatbuilder wandering around boats." Her eyes were wide and she nodded her head in affirmation of her words.

He placed his hand on hers. She let go her grip and let their fingers entwine. He then held her close, and she rested her head against his shoulder. "All right," he said softly. "If it's that important, then I'll do it."

Down at the van, Mary kissed her husband through the open window. Rifkin sat next to him waiting to be taken to the alternative adventure – car travel was usually a good bet in that regard. "You don't have to take the dog, you know," she said, the purpose behind her statement not being lost on Derek.

"Hey, he's a mate," he said. "But don't worry, he won't lead me astray."

"I know that," she replied, looking serious despite his grin. "I just think he might encourage you to…you know…go off on a tangent."

He revved the engine. "He's just a dog, Sweetheart," he replied, still grinning. "And I promise, if we see any tangents, there's no way that we'll be going off on them."

She smiled, just a little, and patted the roof. He

reversed around. Through the open window he took a final sniff of the smells coming from the gully – they were still there – and then, summoning extra resolve, he put the van into first gear and drove off.

Even though it was a Sunday, there were still plenty of boats in the yacht club yard. This was because most of the owners didn't want to take the risk of being caught in some really foul weather that looked like hitting this part of the coast. The northerly was under twenty knots, but several hundred miles to the north-east there was a deep depression forming that could easily turn into a cyclone. It'd been over thirty years since one of these monsters had visited the region around Yuragan but few boaties were taking any chances out in the water. In fact, Derek saw that a few of the trailer sailer owners had already removed their vessels from the yard – probably taking them back to sheds or driveways at home where they thought the risk of damage would be less if the big winds did actually come this way.

Wandering further down the rows, he saw Fergus O'Brien, the caretaker, helping another man to secure a large motor cruiser to its launch trailer with extra ropes and webbing tie-downs. The trailer itself had already been chained and shackled to one of the big, galvanized eyes that poked up from the concreted ground – something that most people never bothered doing in normal circumstances. For a moment, Derek remembered the steel eye that had been so close to his head when he'd fallen from the trestle.

"G'day, Fergus," he called as he approached the vessel.

The caretaker turned around as he pulled down on the truckie's hitch that he'd just made in the rope crossing over the boat's cockpit. "Hello there Derek," he replied. "Good to see you back. How was the funeral?" He finished tying the knot and walked over.

"The what?" Derek said.

"The funeral," Fergus replied. "I heard your apprentice telling one of the members last week that you'd gone to a funeral down near Sydney somewhere."

Derek thought quickly. He'd confided in Jono about the reason for his absence – in general terms at least: 'some government people in Canberra want to check me and my sniffer out,' he'd said, finally admitting to his young charge that there was some truth in the stories about his ability. 'But don't tell anyone else that,' he'd added without offering any alternative – shying away from the idea of lying, as usual.

"Well, that wasn't quite true," he said to his old school mate, knowing he could trust Fergus. "Jono was just protecting me and my privacy." He didn't elaborate, and knew that Fergus wouldn't enquire. "But let me say this; it's good to be back."

They wandered down between the boats, stopping

occasionally to discuss one of the vessels, and looking up at the darkening clouds and wondering aloud whether a cyclone might finally pay a visit after so many years of peace. Rifkin and Woofa, Fergus's dog, had found each other, and the two animals followed the men, sniffing the ground and each other, and playing 'piss on the trailer wheels'.

"We don't usually see you down here on Sundays," Fergus said as he surveyed the skies. "Almost every other day, but not Sundays. You worried about some of ya work blowin' away?"

Derek ran his hand along the hull of a small yacht that he and his father had built together more than twenty-five years ago, one of several still in the yard. "No, the truth is, Mary talked me into coming here today – to get back to my trade roots I s'pose you could say." He turned and faced the caretaker. "It's all a bit fucking complicated, Fergus," he said as looked across at the dogs, both of which were staring, prick-eared, in the direction of the hill next to the boat yard. "This smelling ability that we talked about a while ago – it's got some strange side effects. I don't know if they're good or bad, but they're fucking strange."

"How d'ya mean?" the big man said, fixing his gaze on Derek.

"Well, it's like, I'm constantly being hit with all these new…I dunno…*awarenesses* of what's going on around me – to do with smells and scents, I mean. It's really hard to describe what it's like, Fergus, but it just seems to take up so much of my, my…time, I suppose. I mean, there's so much going on in my brain to do with smells and odours and the images and memories they stir up – there's not a lot of time left for things like…you know, thinking and planning and being careful about stuff. There's just so many distractions goin' up my nose and into my head." He sighed. "Fuck, I don't know if that explains it very well." He leaned against the hull and again looked across at the dogs who were now slowly walking in the direction of the hill.

Fergus hadn't lifted his gaze from Derek's face. "So does it bother you?" he asked. "Would you prefer to not have the ability, to be back how you were?"

Derek slowly shook his head, not as a negative response but in admiration of Fergus's natural insight – hammer right on the fucking nail. "That's the very question I've been asking myself lately," he replied. "On the one hand I can know the world in an amazing way, like nobody else – it's rich and spectacular and so fucking interesting. But on the other hand, I'm just sort of losing interest in things that I've always thought were important, like thinking ideas through, and organizing, and sticking to a job until it's properly finished. And it's more than just losing interest…I'm actually losing the ability to do that sort of stuff."

"No brain time," Fergus said.

"Exactly."

They stood in silence for several seconds, Fergus looking out across the water, and Derek looking up at the hill. Then Fergus spoke. "You'll find the balance, mate," he said, "but I expect it won't be easy; giving up some old and taking on some new – it's bound to be bumpy road, but you'll get there."

Derek shook his head again, and this time he smiled. "Thanks, Fergus, it's nice to hear you say that… You're a smart fucker; you know that, don't you?" he added.

Fergus grinned. But then his expression suddenly changed as he noticed Rifkin and Woofa scampering towards a hole in the fence. "Bloody hell, where are those two goin'?" he said, and then made a piercing whistle using his thumb and forefinger pressed into his lips. Woofa stopped for a moment, looked back at Fergus and then at Rifkin who was still heading towards the base of the hill. You could almost see the big dog's thoughts: friend or master, friend or master. Friend won. "Fucking dog," Fergus said as he started walking towards the gate near the hole.

"There's a dead wild goat up on the hill," Derek said. "And another dog's already up there havin' a go at it." He hurried to join Fergus.

The big man continued walking. "Holy shit, you can tell that?" he said.

"Yeah I knew it when they did," Derek replied. "Come on, I'll show you where they're goin'," he called as he ran ahead.

The smell of rotting goat guts was still in the van as Derek sat and waited for the electrically-operated gate to open. "You stink, Rifkin," he said to his dog. "I'm gunna have to scrub your fuckin' snout when we get home." Rifkin's ears flattened and he lowered his head, pretty much aware that his master wasn't too happy with him. Derek noticed. "Aah, it's all right, I'm not angry with you, ya pongy mongrel," he said, and he reached over and patted the dog while slowly edging the van out of the boat yard.

He was half-way home – just entering a small roundabout on the main road that ran along the coast – when he made a sudden decision, and rather than continuing through the roundabout, he pulled the steering wheel to the left. Rifkin, who had been happily sitting and watching the world through the windscreen fell to the right, and in his scramble to stay upright, scratched Derek's gear-changing left hand with his claws. "Whoa! Sorry fella," Derek said as he slowed down. "Took that one a bit too fast."

The cause of the abrupt diversion was his decision to pay Jono a visit. It wasn't as if he'd been dwelling on anything in particular to do with his apprentice – not that he was aware of anyway. He'd just been enjoying the sights and smells of the ocean when the turn-off to Jono's place appeared, and something caused him to take it. He continued up the hill away from the coast, wondering what was behind the impulse.

As he entered another street, it dawned on him that it might be a good idea to have a heart to heart talk with the young fella – reassure him that things would be all right, even though he – Derek – might be behaving a bit strangely. He forced himself to think a bit further...yes, that was it, that's why he'd almost sent Rifkin flying out the driver's window. He frowned. It was as though his logical thought processes were still working, and that they'd caused him to take action, but that he wasn't aware of the reason until a short time after – action first, justification later. *Jesus*, he thought, as the bizarre nature of the idea struck him, and he wondered whether this was going to be another little distinguishing feature of his evolving mental landscape. Or maybe it was a common effect, that happens to everyone: you do something without any apparent reason at the time, and it's only later that you see what must have been going on in your subconscious. He blew air across his teeth in a noisy sort of sigh; he didn't want to think about it any more – probably couldn't, even if he wanted to.

He made another turn and then pulled up in front of the small fibrocement house that Jono rented from one of his uncles – part of the rental being free maintenance of the guy's boat. Derek couldn't see his apprentice's blue holden ute, but that didn't necessarily mean he wasn't in – the old car seemed to do the rounds of Jono's mates like a bottle of Johnnie Walker at a teenage drinking party. When he opened the van door to get out, Rifkin made a squeaky noise in his throat and stood on the passenger seat ready to jump. Derek hesitated, then said, "Come on then," and Rifkin happily bounded out onto the bitumen.

Before walking down the path to the house, Derek looked across at the tall lemon-scented gums in a vacant block on the other side of the road. The upper parts of their main trunks were bending under the force of the wind – stronger up here than at the yacht club – and the rush of air through the leaves made a swishing sound like when you drag a fallen palm frond along a dry lawn. And the smells being brought by the northerly seemed to be a bit different up here than at sea level; as though some of the marine scents had been filtered out and replaced by earthy smells: wet vegetation, freshly ploughed soil, flowers of the forest – lilly pilly and tulipwood. A storm would surely hit soon.

The front door was closed but Derek could hear music coming from inside – the noise of the wind not yet strong enough to obliterate other sounds; but getting close. He opened the fly-wire screen and knocked loudly on the faded timber panel behind. No one answered so he tried again, but still there was no answer, so he turned and stepped down from the porch. He was halfway up the path when all at once his nose detected a vaguely familiar scent. Despite its subtlety, it was powerful enough to spin him around. At the same time he heard a matching voice – it too, being familiar. "Is that you, Mister Sadler?" it said.

Already, he could feel the blood moving from everywhere else in his body to his face as the scent began to swamp his perceptive processes. He looked back, and saw the reason for his consternation – Jono's girlfriend, Wendy Butler. She was standing in the doorway wearing a sarong tied low around her hips, showing off a small amethyst in her navel; and the briefest of bikini tops – yellow, and barely able to contain her ample young bosom. She was smiling, her eyes blue and happy. "I thought it was you," she said as he walked haltingly towards her, his head swimming.

"Jono's not here – gone to watch his cousin play rugby in Trelby – him and some mates. There was no room for me," she giggled. "But I didn't want to go anyway." She studied Derek's face. "Are you all right, Mister Sadler? You look a bit hot. Why don't you come in and have a drink?"

Derek had trouble thinking – the amethyst vibrated when she laughed, and her voice was soft and sympathetic. But it was her smell that had him by the balls – almost literally. It was sweet and warm and damp and of the sea, and it stirred up images of stroking and kissing and touching and penetrating. He stood in front of her, as stunned as a truckload of dead mullet, his pulse rate heading off the scale.

Every person he'd encountered since the accident had a particular olfactory signature, and women had some components – attractive – that were peculiar to their sex. When they were fertile, ovulating, he could tell, and it added a further pleasantness to a woman's scent. That's how he found it anyway. But there was something about Wendy Butler's secretions, wherever they were coming from, that simply drove him wild. It'd been the case since he first noticed her scent on Jono all those weeks ago just after his fall. Back then he'd worried about what he might do if he actually saw her, and now all those fears had suddenly returned – like bang, right in his face. Try as he might to avoid it, he had an almost overwhelming desire to lay in a cool, secret place with her, and to take in her scent at close quarters; to fondle, to moisten, to exchange fluids.

He blinked several times, and then gave his head a shake. "No, I'm fine," he heard himself say. "I've just been doing a bit of running up a hill after this character." He pointed to Rifkin who was sniffing a nearby patch of marigolds. "I just thought I'd pop in and say hello to Jono, but I can talk to him tomorrow, of course."

He was about to offer a parting word when she hurried down from the porch and took hold of one of his arms. "No, you can't go without having a drink," she said. "I don't want to be responsible for not tending a dehydrated boatbuilder – especially not my boyfriend's boss," and she playfully tugged him towards the front door.

Inside was surprisingly cool…and neater than Derek remembered. Rather than bits of car and outboard engines strewn around the floor, mingling with dirty mugs and plates and old clothes and pizza boxes – as he recalled from previous visits – the little lounge room was now an exemplar of tidiness and good taste. A pine bookshelf now held the magazines and manuals that used to be randomly distributed around the house, and there were framed prints of modern art works hanging on walls that previously held blu-tacked marine charts and posters of football players. These small observations made a minor impact on a very small portion of Derek's brain – the rest was dealing, one way or the other, with the presence of Wendy and her wonderfully beguiling smell.

Still with her hand around his arm, she sat him down on the couch. "Soft or hard?" she asked as she slowly straightened up.

Derek's eyes were focused on her cleavage and the tops of her breasts. He closed his eyes and took a deep breath. It was a bad idea; the massive inhalation of her odour made him want to reach out and take hold of her shoulders, and to gently pull her towards him. He didn't do it, but forcing himself not to took a huge mental effort.

"Mister Sadler?" she said. "Would you like a soft drink or something harder – a beer maybe?"

He opened his eyes; she was frowning now, obviously concerned about his behaviour. "Oh, a glass of water would be good thanks, Wendy," he said. "Cold and simple." He watched the top of her sarong wiggle as she walked away, and he held his breath until she'd disappeared into the kitchen. He wanted to stay and he wanted to go: excited and afraid, hopeful and guilt-ridden.

"Here you are," she said a few minutes later, handing him a large glass of water with ice cubes in it. "That should cool you down."

He looked up and noticed the wisps of blonde hair that had escaped from the large, Polynesian-style hairpin at the back of her head – they framed the sides of her pretty, sun-browned face. She smiled, totally unaware – he was sure – of the nuclear war taking place inside his own head, not to mention his pants. As he accepted the offered glass, their hands brushed against each other. This, together with the pervasiveness of her magical scent, was to be the straw that broke the camel's back; the butterfly that caused the hurricane; the colliding particle that started the atomic chain reaction. He was in the process of standing up, his blind intention being to...he didn't know what...maybe to gently brush the hair from her face before taking her in his arms; or to reach out and stroke her breasts. Somewhere deep inside, the part of him that would normally control his thoughts and actions was screaming, *What the fuck are you doing? Have you lost your fucking mind?* But it no longer had control; the shots were now being called by the part of his brain that evolved long before his ancestors stood upright – flooded with olfactory imperatives, and supported by sight and sound and touch. Then Rifkin saved the day. Saved Derek.

The sound of serious dog screeching and yelping suddenly erupted on the porch. The front door was open, and as Derek dropped his free hand and turned his head, he saw flashes of fur and teeth passing in front of the flywire. He identified Rifkin as one of the combatants, with the other having a dappled brown and cream coat – possibly a German shepherd. He ran across to the flywire door and pushed it open. "Get the fuck out of it," he screamed as he kicked at the other dog – it *was* a German shepherd, and it had Rifkin bailed up in one of the corners formed by the wall of the house and the side of the porch. He also threw his glass of ice water over it for good measure, and quickly grabbed an old chair that was leaning against the rail. The big dog yelped at the impact of Derek's boot, and when it saw he meant business with the chair, it jumped from the porch and ran up the street.

In typical dog fashion, Rifkin found new valour as a result of his pack leader's intervention. He began barking, and started off after the would-be attacker, but Derek grabbed him at the steps. "Oh no you don't," he said. "Don't go pushing ya luck ol' boy."

Wendy was standing at the doorway with a broom in her hand. "Is he all right?" she asked.

"Yeah, he looks okay," Derek replied as he examined his quivering and still-barking companion.

She walked over to the steps and squatted down next to Derek. "Bring him inside and I'll get you another drink," she said, as she stroked Rifkin.

Derek stared at her profile and sniffed – he could've told that she was squatting even if he couldn't see her. God! What was it about her scent? "No," he said with a great deal of reluctance and effort. "I really have to be going."

"Okay," she replied as she stood up and walked over to the door. "I'll tell Jono you dropped by. See ya."

As Derek and his dog walked to the van, it started to piss down with rain.

By the time he arrived home, the heavens had dumped enough water on the land to cause myriad tiny rivulets to course their way down into the drainage ditches on either side of the driveway. Even the short run from the van to the stairs was enough exposure for him to get soaked. "Looks like rain," he shouted as he stepped into the kitchen. But it was a wasted joke, no one was there.

"We're in here," Mary called from the lounge room.

Derek shook the water from his hair, and walked across the floor pulling his wet T-shirt up over his head. "I said…" he began, with his face and arms momentarily tangled up in the wet cotton fabric.

"Yes, we heard you – it looks like rain – very funny," Mary replied from somewhere in front of him.

He struggled with the clinging fabric, twisting and turning and unable to see. "Fucking T-shirt," he said as he gave it a final tug. But even before the garment sprung off over his head, his nose told him who was in the room, and now his eyes confirmed it. Mary was sitting at one end of the couch; she had a cheeky grin on her face that said, *Let's see how you handle this, my man.* At the other end of the couch was Pierce, and across from him – on one of the padded chairs, was Amanda Crowther, the TV producer.

"Jesus! What are you two doing here?" he said as he looked from one to the other. "Did you come together or separately?"

"Separately," Pierce replied, looking uncomfortable. "Quite independently."

"Hi Derek," Amanda said, giving a little wave, with her eyes darting from his face to his bare chest and then back to his face.

"So…what…" He looked down at Mary.

She raised herself from the couch and said, "Why don't I get you a towel and some dry clothes, and we'll leave these people to chat for a moment." Of course, what she was really saying was, *Come with me and I'll explain what seems to be going on.* Pierce and Amanda knew this too, and that she was just being polite.

In the bedroom, Mary spoke in a loud whisper as he wiped himself over with a towel. It was obvious that he couldn't hear her, however, because of the sound of the rain pelting down on the tin roof. "I said they both got here within ten minutes of each other," she repeated, now in a louder than normal voice – which was still only barely audible. "The woman – Amanda – was calling all last week, asking me to pass on details about her TV plans for you." Derek stopped dressing and stared at his wife, his eyebrows raised. "I didn't want to bother you with anything while you were in Canberra," she said. "And then when you got home, you seemed to be worried enough about the government thing, and I was concerned about…you know…the business and your work. I just didn't want to give you yet another hassle to deal with." She handed Derek a dry pair of shorts. "I was going to tell you tonight, but…well…she's here now. I had no idea she was coming – or Pierce. Obviously, they both want to talk to you. She doesn't seem to mind that Pierce is here, but he certainly seems embarrassed."

"So where are their cars?" he said, almost having to shout because of the rain noise.

"The hail," she shouted back. He frowned. "The hail

started just as Amanda arrived. I got her to put her car in the old shed up the back – to protect it; Pierce did the same with his." She saw that Derek was still frowning. "Didn't it hail where you were?"

Derek shook his head, and decided not to mention where he'd been when the rain started – not right now at least. He'd probably have to say something at some stage – the experience with…he was almost too afraid to even think her name…Wendy…worried him to his core. Right now, however, the two people out in the lounge room were a more immediate problem.

"So it's just a coincidence that they're here at the same time?" he said close to her ear as he pulled on a new T-shirt.

"I'm not sure," she shouted back. "I get the impression that Amanda might know something about Pierce. Maybe she followed him here. He went a lighter shade of pale when she told him she was a film producer and that she was going to make a documentary about you."

Derek took a deep breath through his nose. The smells brought on by the rain were extraordinary: some sharp and electric, like the scent of the rhinoceros beetles out in the bush, and others musty and fungal, like the odour of the now-soaked hay that Mary had put around her garden beds at one end of the house. And everything smelled damper, Mary included.

He forced himself back to the issue of his visitors.

"Come on," he said to his wife. "Let's try and sort this out." She was looking up at the ceiling. The noise was now almost deafening, and she'd obviously not heard him, so he took her hand and led her down the passageway.

When they entered the lounge room, Pierce and Amanda were both standing at a window, looking out over the veranda at the deluge beyond. Rather than trying to make himself heard, Derek walked over and touched Pierce on the shoulder. They both turned around, each one obviously a little concerned. But before anyone could speak, young Harry and his big brother, Tim, burst into the room yelling – excited and scared.

"The man on the radio said a cyclone is coming here, Daddy, and it's named Brenda," Harry shouted. He looked at Tim and then back to Derek. "We're not going to die are we?"

Chapter 8

"Just be quiet for a minute, Darling," Mary said to Harry as she pointed the remote at the TV. Since his announcement a short time ago about the cyclone, he'd been flooding her with questions: Where should they go? What should they do? Would there be a flood? Should he put all his toys in a safe place? Would they have to tie each other to some strong point, like in a film he'd seen? Now everyone in the room watched the ghosting figures on the television screen – the images were barely visible, and the dialogue was lost in the harsh hiss of accompanying static.

"Could be our aerial down, or the tower on Mount Billings," Mary said as she flicked through the commercial channels.

"Try the ABC," Derek suggested, "they've got a different set up."

Suddenly, a much clearer picture appeared, still hazy, but easily recognizable. Mary increased the volume, but the Gatling gun sound of the rain on the roof continued to make hearing difficult. They all stared at the screen with its weather map and commentator.

"…now named Cyclone Brenda," the dour-faced man said, "It has taken an unexpected turn towards the coast and is moving at a relatively rapid rate. The eye of Brenda is expected to pass close to the town of Saint Elmo late this evening…"

Derek turned to Pierce and Amanda, "Fifty kay north," he said loudly.

"…but as this bulletin goes to air, surrounding areas are already experiencing rain ahead of the strong winds."

The image changed to that of a familiar newsreader. "Just repeating," she said, "the former depression off the central Queensland coast has now been classified as a category three cyclone, and has been given the name Brenda. People in coastal regions from Bowen to Gladstone are advised to follow the…" then both the image and the sound were all but lost in a freckly, shooshing outburst.

"Oh fuck, great," Derek said, with no thought of apologizing for his language. "Tim, go and get your radio – it's still got batteries in it hasn't it?"

The teenager had a serious-but-excited expression on his face – like a rookie soldier about to take part in his first battle. "Yeah, I just put some in last week," he answered before running off to his bedroom.

"I'm coming too!" Harry called as he broke away from his mother.

Derek turned to his two visitors. Amanda had her mobile phone pressed against one ear and her remaining hand pressed against the other ear. "You two can't even think about leaving at this stage," he said to Pierce who had been frowning for the last five minutes.

"I wouldn't even be able to find my way down to the road in this rain," he replied.

At the same time, Amanda took the phone from her ear and stared down at its screen. She then looked across at the two men. "Can't get through," she said, looking more annoyed than worried.

"The network's probably overloaded," Pierce offered, and then added, "It looks like we'll be here for the duration." She glanced at Derek and he nodded in agreement.

"But I've got a schedule..." She trailed off as she looked out the window, and heard the rain noise go up a notch.

Derek's brain was still presenting him with a multitude of new and modified smell images brought on by the wind and water, but he wrested himself free of their dominance. "Look, everybody," he shouted – noticing the two boys returning to the room with Tim's radio. "All this rain is just the beginning – the introduction. The noise it's making right now is gunna start changing soon, seem to get less. But that's only because it'll be getting more horizontal – won't be hitting the roof in the same way; and it'll start pounding against the windows and the walls. But at that stage, it'll be the sound of the wind that takes over – the rain'll seem like bugger all."

"I locked up the workshop, and threw a whole lot of loose stuff into the far end of the garage," Mary said. "… hoses, sprinklers, bits of wood, bricks, old chairs…"

"Oh, shit! What about the spray-painting screen," Derek interrupted as he lowered his head trying to see out the window and into the greyness beyond the veranda. "It'll take off like a fucking hang-glider," he added without thinking.

"Unpegged it and put it away," Mary said.

He quickly turned back to her and grinned – *what a woman*, he thought. However, the grin promptly disappeared as she continued.

"But there are still those sheets of roofing iron from the old chook pens lying around the back. Remember, Andy Medelson's been promising to come and get them for months."

"Come on Pierce, Tim," Derek said. "We'll have to tie 'em down."

Tim looked surprised but obviously delighted – his dad having chosen him for an urgent and important job. Harry, on the other hand was clearly unhappy. "What about me?" he protested as the others followed his father towards the door.

Derek stopped and looked back. "We need you to help

Mum and Amanda to check all the windows, and to use towels to seal up the bottoms of the doors that open onto the veranda or to outside. And you have to get torches and candles and lanterns and matches and other stuff that Mum asks you for – and put it all in here. In fact, I want you to be in charge of getting it all together." He looked across at Mary, winked, and then strode into the kitchen.

Pierce stood in the workshop, water dripping from the cheap, hooded rain jacket Derek had given him. "Tell me again why you're drilling the holes?" he yelled into the boatbuilder's ear – the noise blasting down from the workshop's bare tin roof making speech almost impossible.

"To put the chain through," Derek yelled back as he pulled down on the drill-press arm. "Lucky I had these four-be-two stakes, otherwise we'd have to cut the fuckers from scratch, and we're running out of time – that wind is starting to pick up."

Tim hurried across from a tool rack carrying a sledgehammer and a medium-sized, boltcutter. "Mister, umm…"

"Pierce, call me Pierce."

The boy nodded. "There's another sledge hammer over there," he shouted, pointing, "…and the bucket of chain. Would you give me a hand?"

Ten minutes later, the three were running towards a

raised, flat area at the back of the house – their flimsy raincoats offering little protection from the downpour. Derek dropped his armful of short, hardwood stakes, and the bolt cutter, next to the pile of roofing iron. The half dozen or so bricks already sitting on the top sheet were lifting slightly with each gust of the increasing wind. "Jesus," he said to himself, realizing that they would have to work fast to stop the four metre lengths of iron from becoming airborne – and lethal. Then he paused for a moment and sniffed. "Oh, Christ," he said as the others arrived. "Put the bucket on top," he yelled to Pierce. "And be careful, there's a fucking snake somewhere under the tin." Pierce suddenly stopped. "Don't worry," Derek shouted, "it'll be too fuckin' scared to come out," and then added under his breath, "I hope." He then picked up one of the stakes, stuck its point into the ground beside the roofing iron, and began tapping it with the head of one of the sledgehammers. Once the stake was in place, he stood up and continued to thump it until it was deeply embedded in the wet earth – like a giant tent peg. "You do the same on the other side," he yelled to Pierce as he gave a couple of final taps. "We'll put two separate lengths of chain across, and one from end to end." Without speaking, Pierce picked up three stakes and hurried around to the other side of the pile of metal sheets.

Derek looked around and saw Tim next to him holding one end of the thin-gauge chain, the other end still buried somewhere in the bucket under hundreds of its galvanized sister links. "Put it through the hole," he called, pointing to the stake. The rain was starting to sting now when it struck them in the face, and the swish of the tree branches and the rattling cacophony from the nearby house roof were being joined by a low, howling sound that seemed to come from all directions at once.

Derek reached into his pocket and pulled out a small shackle. He then knelt down next to his son, and while Tim held the end of the chain, Derek shackled it to the standing part that drooped down from the bucket. "Good man," he yelled. "Now pull out a length that we can pass through the stake on the other side; I'll cut it with these." He picked up the boltcutter, and felt for the other shackles in his pocket.

Pierce was still hammering in stakes, and Derek and Tim had just attached one end of the second length of chain when a huge gust whipped through the area where they were working. The bucket of chain – still sitting on top of the pile but now also filled with water – tumbled over as the ends of the top few sheets lifted in the air – fanning up like giant pages in a book, and only stopped from becoming airborne by the piece of chain they had already put in place. Several of the bricks also flew off, one barely missing Pierce as he ran towards them. "You two finish this one while I do the lengthwise one," Derek yelled while snipping through the chain. "We have to get inside." He handed Tim a shackle and then rushed to the end of the pile.

Several minutes later, another big gust hit, but this time the sheets of roofing iron hardly moved – held down by the crisscross of chain. The plastic bucket, however, now devoid of its contents, was swept up towards the treetops – lost in the wind-blasted landscape and the gathering darkness. Derek quickly moved around the anchor points tightening the shackle shafts with a pair of pliers he'd brought. Tim followed him with the sledgehammer, giving each stake a few final belts in order to pull the chains tighter.

After storing the tools back in the workshop, Tim and Pierce waited while Derek drove the van into the adjoining garage. The three of them then struggled with the old hinged doors and locked them shut. "Okay, let's get the fuck outa here," Derek said as he slid the metal bolt into its housing.

Rifkin walked around the kitchen barking and dog talking with excitement, obviously happy at the return of his owner. "He could see you through the back window," Mary said as she handed each of the waterlogged three a towel. "He's been whining ever since you left." She paused in front of Tim and smiled, but then looked across to Derek. "Please don't go out there again," she added. It was as much a command as a request.

"Don't worry, this is now staying-in time," he replied. "I just didn't want to be responsible for that roofing iron decapitating some poor bugger further down the coast." He ruffled his hair with the towel and, for the first time, found himself dwelling on the subtle differences in the scents of the other two males. The soaking had caused their signature odours to be overlayed with something that was…heavier, and more ammonia-like, it seemed. He began to explore the individual components, fascinated by the new interactions.

"Daddy?" It was Harry.

Derek blinked, and began ruffling his hair again. "G'day, Harry," he said. "Did you get all the torches and lamps into the lounge room?"

"Did he what," his mother said. "It was like a military operation."

Harry pulled at his father's hand to come look, but Derek remained where he was. "In a minute, mate," he said sternly. He then stared into Mary's eyes, searching for emotions that she may not otherwise reveal. Her scent gave no hint of fear, just resolution. "Is everything okay here?" he asked, his voice raised.

She nodded. "We've blocked up the bottoms of the doors with towels and rags, put big Xs of masking tape across all the windows, and closed all the curtains. We've also got water and food and blankets in the lounge room next to Harry's 'cyclone cubby'." She paused as Amanda entered the kitchen, and listened with the others as the low howl outside slowly built up to a higher frequency – higher than before – and then dropped down again. She shivered. "I just wish we had storm shutters," she shouted.

"We will after this, believe me," Derek replied, giving her arm a gentle squeeze. He then walked over to a cabinet and took something out of one of its drawers. Next, he clapped his hands to get everyone's attention. "Okay, we're as ready as we can be," he said loudly to the staring faces as he held up two decks of playing cards. "The Sadler Games Centre is now open."

An hour or so later Derek, Pierce, and Amanda were sitting on the floor around a low coffee table – cards in their hands. Mary was next to them, dozing on the couch – with little Harry sprawled out, all arms and legs, and fast asleep, on top of her. Tim was sitting, knees up, on one of the nearby lounge chairs. He had his eyes closed but his occasional head movement showed that he was still listening to Trelborough HOTFM through the ear plugs – music most of the time, but with regular Cyclone Brenda notices. Up until a few minutes earlier, Rifkin had been stretched out on the floor next to Derek but was now over at the curtains, sniffing.

Rain was still pouring down from the skies, still making a thunderous clatter on the roof, but it was the sound of the wind that now predominated – just as Derek had predicted. There was a constant roar, but this was accompanied by a screeching sound that every now and then would slowly increase in frequency and volume until it seemed like something must follow: an explosion or a great gong or a fanfare of heavenly trumpets…a climax; anything. But it never came. Instead, the intensity and pitch would continue to increase, well beyond what you thought possible, and your anxiety level – the anticipation that something disastrous must soon happen – would rise in unison. If you didn't control this, it threatened to burst your brain. And then the screech would die off, and everyone would breathe easy.

"What did you say this game was called?" Amanda asked as the screeching dropped back to the steady roar.

"Dublinet," he said as he tossed down one card and scooped it back up with several others.

"And you say it's from the Balkans?" she replied.

"Well, it was a Croatian guy who showed it to me, and he said he played it as a kid in the old country. Why, do you reckon it should be Irish?"

The other two laughed, and then abruptly stopped as he placed down an ace and took all the other cards from the table. "Retska," he cried.

Pierce looked across at Amanda, and then at Derek. "Are you sure you're not smelling our cards?" he said.

"Yes," Amanda agreed, smiling, "that would explain why you've been winning so many tricks."

Derek chuckled, but noted that it was the first time he'd heard his visitors openly mention his ability while they were together. "Actually, some of the cards do have different odours," he replied, "but I'm consciously trying not to remember which is which." The other two stared at him with bemused expressions. "No, really," he said.

They played another round in silence, and then Amanda spoke without looking up from her hand. "So, tell me Pierce," she said, "what, exactly, is your interest in Derek's extraordinary smelling capability?"

Derek grinned, firstly because he admired how she'd come right out of the blue with such a well-focused question – he knew that as a documentary maker, she must have been dying to find out more about Pierce's involvement and that she'd obviously been waiting for the right moment to pop the question. Secondly, he thought it might be entertaining to see how the academic-cum-senior-public-servant would answer the question.

Pierce rested his cards facedown on the table. "There's not a lot to tell," he said, lying as smoothly as a professional con man. "Derek and I are friends, and he has told me about his new…skill." Derek maintained his grin, wondering where this would go, and noticing a slight change in the scent coming from Pierce.

"Nice try," Amanda replied after making a little laugh, "but I happen to know that you're in charge of some sort of special task force set up by the prime minister's department, and that you've just had Derek down in Canberra for a week." Pierce stared at her, the surprise on his face lasting for a couple of seconds. Then he frowned and puckered his lips to one side – obviously thinking about how to respond. But Amanda continued. "I used to be an investigative journalist," she said, "…still am to some extent; and I've got quite a few contacts."

Pierce sighed, and lowered his head. He might've said something quietly but the others couldn't hear anything above the continuing roar outside. "Come on, Pierce," Amanda goaded, "I've told you I'm a documentary maker, and that Derek has agreed to give us exclusive rights to his smell story, so why don't you come clean with me, so we can be accurate in what we say about you and the government." Derek could detect a change in her odour too – something slightly pungent, like nutmeg – she was on the attack.

"I don't think you'll be mentioning either me or the government's interest in Derek in your documentary," Pierce responded, his head now raised.

"What, you think you can get a court order stopping me?" she replied.

Pierce nodded, obviously surprised at the young blonde's astuteness in anticipating him.

"You would only be able to do that on the basis of national security," she continued. "So, what, have you been testing whether Derek can home in on weapons of mass destruction? Or finding backyard bomb factories; that sort of thing?"

Pierce didn't answer, his expression stoic. On the other hand, Derek couldn't help himself; he turned his head back and forth in a sign of admiration, and smiled. This girl was good…and relentless.

"Come on Pierce," she said again. "I don't want to be your enemy. Tell me what's going on – in general terms if you like – and I'll stay away from names and details. Jesus, anyone who sees the doco is going to assume the government will have talked to Derek anyway, even if we say nothing about it. People aren't totally stupid you know – not all of them."

"Not all at the same time, at least," Derek added. Amanda looked at him and laughed. He liked her smell, and the subtle changes it had been going through.

Pierce raised his shoulders and then let them drop. "Okay, let me be straight with you," he said. "At this stage Derek isn't an official secret, so information about him or his activities to date aren't covered by the Commonwealth Crimes Act – except, that is, for his work with the government last week, where he was employed as a consultant. So, at this time, I can't see any problem with you doing your documentary, but neither he nor I can talk to you about what happened last week. However, you're obviously very smart, and can draw your own general conclusions. But I would ask you to exercise a high level of responsibility in regard to national security. Also, if Derek begins working for us full time, you may find it a lot more difficult to make any sort of documentary about him."

She turned to Derek. "So, are you going to be a full-time terrorist sniffer working in secret for the government, or are you going to keep your freedom and probably become famous?"

"I don't think that represents the situation very accurately," Pierce said, looking towards the curtains as the outside banshee screech began its climb in pitch yet again.

"Neither of you know the half of it," Derek said, his voice raised higher than before – partly to make himself heard, and partly because he was angry that both these people, friendly as they were, had no idea of the many personal issues affecting him as a result of his hyperosmia. To each of them he was simply a useful commodity, something that would make them more successful in their respective careers. They could argue all they fucking liked about who could say what about him, and who might use him in what way. But he would decide what he was going to do – no one else – and his decision would be based on the issues as he saw them.

It was just after two in the morning when the tree fell through the house. Everyone except Derek had been sleeping fitfully since before midnight: Harry and Mary still on the couch, Tim still in his chair, and Pierce and Amanda next to each other on foam mattresses Harry had dragged in earlier from his bedroom. Derek hadn't been able to sleep at all – not even doze. The sounds made by Brenda had combined with the onslaught of new aromas to keep his mind buzzing, like being strung out on caffeine. Every half hour or so, he'd stop playing patience, or put down the newspaper he'd been trying to read by lamplight (the power having gone off sometime earlier), and go for a wander around the house, Rifkin by his side. Together they would check out each room, both visually and osmatically, and Derek would ring out soaked towels at the bottoms of doors and windows, and position buckets and ice cream containers so they would catch drips from various parts of the ceiling. Occasionally, they'd hear scurrying up in the roof cavity, and this would confirm what their noses were already telling them: that a menagerie of mammals, birds, and reptiles was taking refuge above their heads.

He'd just settled himself back in his chair and adjusted the wick on the kerosene lamp, when he heard what seemed like a distant cracking sound – audible above Brenda's roar. This lasted for several seconds and was followed by an unholy crash that filled the room.

Almost instantaneously, everyone was on their feet – except for Harry who continued to sleep despite some unintentional rough handling by Mary.

"What the hell was that?" Amanda yelled, holding a hand to her chest.

Derek didn't say anything straight away but grabbed the big torch and shone it around the room, first on each person and then on the ceiling. Everyone seemed okay – scared, but okay – and there didn't appear to be any damage inside.

Mary grabbed Derek's arm. "The tamarind tree," she said, referring to a huge old tree that had been on the property since well before she and Derek had arrived, and which dominated an area out the back, across from their bedroom.

Derek ran from the lounge room already knowing that his wife was right. The long pods containing the tamarind fruits hadn't yet formed, but their characteristic smell filled his nostrils anyway.

He was only able to push the bedroom door half-open. The torch beam showed a thick branch sticking down through a crumpled section of the ceiling, bits of plaster and smaller branches littering the bed and the floor. The side window was smashed, and a wall of leaves and twigs was poking through the frame. Water was coming through here too, as well as running down the main, penetrating branch.

Derek felt Mary against his back. He turned around; Tim was there too, and Pierce – all wide eyed. "Doesn't look too bad," he said. "I think the main part of the trunk missed the house – but we got a side branch though the roof." He looked down at the water starting to run out from the room. "Tim, go and get grandad's old brace and bit off the wall in the lounge room."

In less than a minute, the young teenager returned with the old boring tool that had made its transition from implement to ornament decades ago. Derek took it from him and at the same time handed Mary the torch. "Just shine it on the floor, Sweetheart," he yelled as raindrops hit his face. "I want to be sure the lowest point is here, near the door."

"Shouldn't the floor be level?" Pierce called from behind.

"Jesus, go back to chemistry," Derek whispered loudly into his wife's ear while continuing to survey the polished wood floorboards.

He then smiled as he heard his son call "It's an old house, Pierce; nothing's level anymore."

Seconds later, Derek was on his knees in about a centimetre of water, cranking the handle of the brace. "You beauty!" he yelled. "Biting into the wood like it was made yesterday." He looked up at the others; they were all grinning. He savoured the scent of the aged tallowwood, diminished but not completely obliterated by the wetness.

After two more holes, no more water was passing beyond the towels rolled up at the bottom of the doorway

– most of it now pouring down the newly made outlets. "No more we can do here," he called, pulling the door shut. "Let's get back to the cubby." He then stopped, suddenly realizing that he didn't have to shout so loud. The others noticed it too.

"Dad, I think the wind's dropping…"

"And the rain is easing," Pierce added.

Derek put his arm around Mary's shoulder. "Yep, we've turned the corner, I'd say. If it dies down as quickly as it built up then I reckon we'll be looking at Brenda's arse by first light." They all smiled, and Mary shook her head in mock disdain.

It was just before six o'clock when Derek rose from his chair and walked over to one of the windows. He peeked through the curtains first, and then pulled them apart. Sunlight filled the room. Even more entered as he did the same at the next window. The sound of the wind was gone, and the rain had stopped.

Tim sat up and stretched, and then reached over to his Walkman radio. He pulled out the ear-plug jack and turned up the volume on the internal speakers. The others stirred. No one spoke while they listened to the various announcements about the cyclone's movements and the trail of destruction it had left in the area. It had remained a category three – which meant winds of up to 224 kilometres per hour – and had dumped 220mm of rain in the Yuragan area over the last ten hours. The damage seemed to be widespread, with trees uprooted, powerlines down, and roofs taken off some buildings. There was a lot of local flooding, and the road to Trelborough was still cut. But much of the actual coastline had escaped the effects of the storm surge because it had been low tide when Brenda was at her peak.

"Thank Christ for that," Derek said when he heard the last piece of news.

"The same goes for it staying a category three," Pierce said as he felt the stubble on his chin. "Last night I was sure it must have gone up a level – Tracy was a four you know, and it obliterated Darwin."

"Yeah, well let's see what Brenda's done around here," Derek replied as he opened the double doors onto the veranda. Rifkin, who had been sitting on the floor trying to dig into his ear with a hind paw, suddenly stopped his preening, and ran out through the opening. There were probably a number of reasons for this but Derek knew that one of them was the jumble of scents and odours that had rushed into the room – snippets of information that tantalized and excited, and that pleaded for further investigation.

Derek stepped through the doorway but stopped when he heard Harry's voice. "Daddy," the boy called as he jumped from the couch. "Wait for me." They walked hand-in-hand onto the veranda; the others followed.

"There's quite a few trees down," Mary said as she surveyed the water-soaked property. She leaned over the railing and looked to the right. "But the workshop and garage look fine – the roofs are still there, and the drains seem to have stopped any flooding."

"The old shed where Amanda and I parked our cars still seems to be intact too," Pierce said, standing on his tiptoes. "Although we can't see it all from here." He looked back at Amanda but she was busy pressing keys on her mobile phone.

Rifkin had already rocketed down the side steps, and they could see him wandering around on the sodden ground below, stopping and sniffing at fallen branches and trees, and around the outbuildings. A gentle breeze drifted towards them, and Derek noticed Rifkin looking up, his nose pointed towards the gully. Derek understood why: there were a lot of unusual odours coming from there, a number of them carrying messages of death. "Drowned animals," Derek said quietly and without thinking.

Mary squeezed his hand. "Sweetheart, why don't you go and see what the tamarind tree has done to the outside of the house."

Derek's attention quickly refocused. "Fuck! The tamarind tree!" he said, feeling a sharp jab of embarrassment. "Of course...I..." He looked at Tim, and then at the others. "Come on, let's see what that bugger has done."

As he descended the steps from the veranda, Amanda came up behind him. "Derek," she whispered, "I don't know if you've had a chance to think about what you want to do regarding the government, but remember, we have a verbal agreement about exclusive rights to your story."

Derek kept walking, he was surprised and becoming irritated. Jesus, they had just come through a cyclone together, and he was about to check out the tree that had fallen on his house. Couldn't this fucking wait? But he said nothing.

"I've just got through to my office, and I really need to get back to Sydney," she went on, "but I don't want to leave without getting something in writing signed by you. It only needs to be..." She stopped when he turned and faced her, his eyes showing his annoyance.

"Amanda," he said in a low voice, barely opening his mouth. "I've got more important things to do right now." He stared at her for a moment as the others came down the steps. "Now, you can either stay here and help out, or you can hop in your car and try getting back to Trelborough, but don't fucking hassle me about signing anything – not today."

The documentary maker's first impulse was to argue, but she read his face and decided against it. "I'll stay," she said. Derek nodded and then continued to walk around the side of the house. She dropped behind the others, and again started pressing keys on her mobile.

The tamarind tree had been huge when standing, and now it appeared even bigger lying on the ground. The giant mass of earth around its upended roots looked like a small island that had been skewered by a gigantic spear shaft, and the tangled assortment of branches up against the house was like a surrealistic extension growing out of the building, with weirdly angled raw-timber beams, and masses of thin-leafed thatching. Luckily, only one of the secondary branches had gone through the roof, buckling the surrounding corrugated-iron sheets. Smaller branches had smashed through the window, and the guttering above had been crushed and was now hanging down from the eaves.

"Could've been a lot worse," Derek said to Mary. "It must've scared the shit out of the animals sheltering in the roof cavity when it hit." He lifted his head and inhaled briefly. "There seem to be a few still around," he added.

"I suppose you'll have to wait until an insurance assessor looks at this before you can sort it out," Pierce said as he took several steps back in order to get a better view of the scene.

"Oh yeah, sure," Derek replied. He then turned to Mary. He was about to speak when he caught a whiff of Amanda's scent. She had just walked past him and was tentatively looking through the jumble of branches. He then noticed the scents of all the others – each now a little different to what it had been during the night when they were trapped in the house together. The open air, and the all-pervading earthy dampness, and the pleasant odour of the tamarind tree; these were all partners in the odiferous dance that was taking place with the personal scents of the people around him. He couldn't help but to concentrate on, to analyse, to savor, the delicate changes.

"What were you going to say, Sweetheart?" Mary said gently.

"Umm…I was going to say…umm…" He thought hard. "The camera, that's it. Would you get the camera. We'll get some shots of the damage."

"I can take the shots," Amanda said, walking back from the tree. "It'll make me feel useful."

"Come on then," Mary said, "We'll get it together."

As the two women walked off around the house, Pierce sidled up to Derek, his eyes following Amanda's wiggling posterior. "She's very pretty, isn't she?" he said. "And intelligent."

"You're talking about Mary, aren't you?" Derek replied, smiling.

"No…I mean yes…I mean, of course…but no, I meant Amanda,"

"Well get your mind off that for now," Derek said, still smiling. "I'm gunna need your help carrying a ladder and chain saw and a few other bits and pieces around here from the workshop." He looked past Pierce and saw Tim and Harry with Rifkin playing around at the root end of the fallen tree. "Come on fellas," he yelled. "We've got a job to do."

Twenty minutes later he was standing on the roof with an arm around the angled branch that had bent and ripped through the corrugated iron. "Here, get a picture of this, Amanda," he called.

"You be careful up there," Mary called back as the blonde next to her raised the Minolta to her eye.

Derek waved, and then pulled the wrecking bar from the tool belt around his waist. He looked down and saw Pierce standing on the ladder, his head and shoulders just above the gutter line. "Hey mate, I'd get right away from there if I were you," Derek said. "If something comes sliding down from up here, you'll be fucked." Pierce touched his forehead in acknowledgment and started back down the ladder. "Just keep everyone away from under here," Derek called to the disappearing head. "Including the dog."

The branch was close to three-quarters of a metre wide where it had gone through the roof. Two adjacent sheets of iron had deformed and been torn apart as a result of the massive impact, and this had affected a number of other sheets near the entry point. Several roof battens were partly visible, and he knew that some of them must have broken, but the mangled sheets were pressed around the branch and it was impossible to see the extent of any damage to the roof frame. A gentle breeze whispered over

Derek's back as he locked the straight end of the wrecking bar under a section of the corrugated iron. He pulled up on the other end of the tool with his gloved hands, and part of the roofing sheet lifted, but not enough to move it out of the way. After pulling a few nearby nails, he tried again, but before levering up on the bar, he felt that cool breeze on his back again. It was bringing some strange and intriguing odours to his nose – marine smells: seaweed and shellfish, mixed with the scents of flowers: frangipani and honeysuckle; and people and animals and things that he couldn't recognize. It was as though that simple little zephyr was a courier for a whole new panorama of wonderful aromas. He stood up and faced into the breeze, eyes closed, nose sampling, brain imaging. As had occurred before, it was as though he'd been transported to another reality – one of fascination and delight.

"Derek! Are you all right?" It was Mary's voice – penetrating his dream-like state. He opened his eyes and looked down towards the ground. Mary and the boys were there – well away from the tree – as were Amanda and Pierce. Tim was holding Rifkin who let out a single bark. Derek waved and then turned back to the operation he had begun. He grabbed hold of the exposed wrecking bar end and put all his strength into lifting it. This time a section of the roofing against the branch came free and he was able to fold part of it back. He leaned forward to look inside the roof cavity, and then suddenly started to draw back – his nose and brain having issued a warning. But it was too late, a flash of brown and yellow shot towards his face: a small, open mouth showing fangs was at the front. "Snake!" he yelled as he instinctively lifted his hands for protection.

He heard Mary scream as he fell backwards, and he smelled the tamarind oils that were released as he crashed through the canopy of leaves. Then all was darkness.

Epilogue

Derek bit into the hamburger, the tomato sauce running down his hand. "You sure you've got enough dead 'orse on that, mate?" Slinky Robinson called from one of the many small groups standing on the grass. Heads turned, and a few people laughed.

"At least I've still got me own teeth, you old bugger," Derek called back, licking his hand. More people laughed. He grinned and then wandered over to the esky to get another stubbie. After that he headed for one of the empty chairs. To tell the truth, he was a bit worn out by all the socializing. He and Mary hadn't had a do like this for quite a while, and even though he was happy enough, he'd never been much of a party animal. Right now, for instance, he was itching to go and do a little more work on the new catamaran frame he'd started to set up in the workshop a week ago. It was such a sweet design, and he really wanted to try out a few of the refined construction ideas he'd come up with.

But he knew the barbecue was a good idea too – one of Mary's in this case. It seemed like a nice way to celebrate the survival of all their friends and neighbours from the cyclone of three weeks ago, and to thank everyone for their support while he was in hospital – again – for those couple of days. 'Derek the Fallen' is what a few of the dags at the marina had started calling him, but he knew it wouldn't last – or hoped it wouldn't, at least.

He leaned back and stared up at the sky, and then slowly cast his eye around the gathering. Richard Barrington, the doctor, was there – talking with Fergus O'Brien from the yacht club. And there was Amanda, involved in some animated discussion with Pierce. He was surprised that either of them had come, given their busy schedules, and the fact that he would be of no use to them any more. Perhaps they were mainly here because of each other rather than as an act of friendship towards him. It was a cynical thought, but he didn't feel overly guilty for having it.

He sighed. If anything, nostalgia was the feeling that filled his spirits at the moment more than anything else. He looked again at the chatting and laughing groups – at the individuals – and he sniffed the air. But he could detect almost nothing; none of the fascinating signature scents that had been so much a part of his life up until only a few weeks ago. He then noticed Rifkin wandering amongst the crowd, picking up scraps from the grass. The dog stopped his food hunt for a moment and looked across at Derek, his snout in the air. Again, Derek couldn't smell anything – except for the burnt meat on the nearby barbecue. Rifkin turned away, and a small wave of sadness swept through his owner.

Certainly, the gift had had its down sides: the declining ability to plan, the loss of motivation to persist with a job, the reduced power of concentration – all because of his growing pre-occupation with smells. And, of course, there was the overwhelming nature of some scents; odours that had the potential to make him do things that might get him into trouble. He had begun to question the other so-called drawbacks, but this last one had been a real problem – had worried him the most.

Mary walked over and squatted down beside his chair. "You're looking a bit lonely over here," she said. "Is everything okay?"

He looked into her concerned eyes and smiled. "Yeah, everything's all right. I just miss…you know… sometimes…"

She reached up and put her arms around his neck. "I know," she said. "But let me tell you this. You might not be a super smeller any more, but you have taken something from the experience – something good." He raised his eyebrows. "I mean you're…more sensitive." She let go one of her arms, and turned to look at their sons.

Tim was piggybacking Harry around the lawn – the little one squealing with delight. "You're now spending more time with the boys," she said and, leaning close to his ear whispered, "And you're an even better lover than before." She then gave him a quick kiss on the cheek and jumped to her feet. "Come on," she said. "Let's go and talk to the others."

Derek was following Mary towards one of the groups when someone tapped him on the shoulder. He turned and was confronted by the smiling face of Wendy Butler. It was the first time he'd seen her since their encounter on the day of the cyclone. "Hello Mister Sadler…I'm sorry, Derek," she giggled. "Would you like one of these cheesy things?" She was holding a plate of hors d'oeuvres.

He grinned. She was still beautiful: blonde, brown-skinned, blue-eyed – and, he couldn't help but confirm – big breasted. But he smelt nothing – nothing at all. "No, thanks, Wendy," he said. "I've had all I need," and he turned and continued to follow his wife.

Lightning Source UK Ltd.
Milton Keynes UK
08 December 2009

147254UK00001B/34/P